# Maggot Girl: Episode 2

Snuff Porn Holocaust

Otis Bateman

*WARNING: Mature content intended for mature audiences only. This is an extreme horror novel that includes scenes of graphic sexual abuse and violence against women and children.*

Edited & formatted by: 360Editing (a division of Uncomfortably Dark Horror).

Editors: Candace Nola. Mort Stone. Darcy Rose.

## Dedication

Dedicated to the fans of Morticia, now forever known as the Maggot Colony. Let's burrow into the carcass and feed! Shoutout to Dakota Dawe and Lindsay Crook. Thanks for the extra eyes, critiques, and constant positivity!

# Contents

# Shall We Begin?

"I Am The Devil, And I Am Here To Do The Devil's Work."
Otis Driftwood

"I Imagine Her Naked, Murdered, Maggots Burrowing, Feasting on Her Stomach, Tits Blackened By Cigarette Burns, Libby Eating This Corpse Out." Patrick Bateman – American Psycho

# Preface

Dear Constant Reader...sorry, I couldn't resist that, I dig me some old SK! You may be asking yourself right now, "Morticia, why the fuck are you writing this instead of that brilliant and handsome writing Phenom Otis Bateman?" Well, it's simple, he is being a total pussy right now, and is more interested in being a mopey, lazy fuck instead of being my would-be autobiographer. Sheesh, what a selfish prick, right??? I mean I get bombarded daily with people wanting to read more of my exploits, and we have this morose motherfucker not writing a single thing in over six months. I mean; shit or get off the proverbial pot, bro!!!!

With Bateman temporarily out of the picture, I thought I would take a stab (HA!) at it and see what would happen. Turns out I'm like the Ernest Hemingway of Splatterpunk, except with titties! Gone are the days of me stuffing my poon with maggot encrusted rotten meat and getting sepsis on the regular. Why keep putting myself in the hospital and almost killing myself? I decided to point my abhorrent cruelty and sadism towards others instead of little ole me. And I've never looked back!

First thing I did was start gathering a plethora of likeminded sycophants to pump up my fragile ego. It wasn't hard to do that since my exploits engulfed the internet worse than the fires in California. I became a fricking legend on the interwebs, dammit. I'm known to many on the darker parts of the web as the Gore Whore. I guess getting my hands covered in the red stuff does get my engine revving, so the moniker is somewhat apt! Next, as a collective whole, we decided that an Only fans account would be a fun way for everyone to enjoy my exploits in a broader way. But instead of sex, this viscera vixen is peddling MURDER! Also, I felt it would be way too tacky to massacre women. I mean, we get enough of that from movies and real life already, so I've made it a point to only butcher the fellas. Sorry, not sorry! That's right, chumps, if you've got a dick, it's open season on your asses! I was a tinge bit nervous my fan base would protest but they were happy if I was happy. Most just wanted bloodshed, gender be damned! It's funny when you become a "celeb" and allow a window's view into your life, you know?

I have all kinds of followers, from nerds and chicks, neck-beards and incels. I also lucked out and get some eggheaded whiz kid help with utilizing VPN (Virtual Private Network) using a Tor browser and set me up with a sweet, encrypted email service. It only cost me a year's membership to my services, and I had that geek at my beck and call! Tonight, will mark the third episode of my Snuff Spectacular, and each one has grown exponentially bigger in terms of viewers and spectacle. I'm not the only one out there profiting off torture porn, far from it. I would like to think I use the quality over quantity approach but I'm also a lazy ass bitch sometimes! I've heard from my followers that my main competition, "Sicko Simon", leaves me in the dust in terms of murders, but they also put no real thought into the butchering of human carcasses like I do. One of their episodes was a homage to Isis, for fucks sake, and all they did was cut off a bunch of ladies' heads; talk about Boresville, USA: ZZZZZ! Little did I know that really big things were heading my way, but even I had no idea what was about to transpire after tonight...

So, now that I've caught all of you lovely readers up to speed on my whereabouts, let the episode begin!

# Chapter One

# The Cam Show From Hell

My palms are sweating in anticipation for tonight's antics. The chatroom for the evening's festivities is absolutely buzzing with malevolent glee for the carnage that is only moments away. Earlier in the week, I created a poll on how my adoring fans wanted my next victim to shuffle off this mortal coil. Some of my more vanilla fans voted for throat slitting, gunshot to the head and strangulation, you know, boring shit like that. But thankfully, most of my fan base has an unquenchable thirst for extreme and inventive bloodshed, and you best bet that I'm here to deliver the grisly goods Goddammit!

As I peruse the different methods to dispatch my upcoming victim that my lovely and resourceful "Maggot Colony" fanatics have sent my way, I come across a truly interesting idea that I'm immediately excited to perform. It is, of course, sent by my number one fan, Travis.

"Jesus, Travis, that is a fantastically vicious way to snuff someone out and I love it!"

I murmur aloud. His choice of murder is stoning or lapidation. Stoning in its purest form, is a kind of capital punishment where you hurl stones repeatedly at your victim, eventually killing them by blunt force trauma. It is popular in Islam where it is referred to as *Rajm* and is the prescribed punishment for adultery under Sharia Law. Which, ironically, is just what this piece of shit loser I'm about to destroy is guilty of.

Another top fan of mine, Rayne, if I recall, had reached out earlier in the week requesting that her friend's boyfriend, Tanner, become a victim on my murder show. Apparently, he has done nothing but cheat on, beat, and verbally assault her friend nearly the entire duration of their relationship. The fan is terrified that her friend is going to die by Tanner's hands and begged me to intervene with my special brand of justice. God, with a name like that it's almost a requisite that he was born to be a human turd and douche sandwich.

After some thought and deliberation, I decided to nab the prick and make him the star for tonight's activities. And just like every other lunkheaded, walking boner I've murdered on the internet, all I had to do was give him the idea that he would get to fuck me by the end of the night, and he was putty in my murderous hands. After we had gone out for dinner, I invited him to my place which he, of course, accepted with zero hesitation. Even after we arrived at my Killzone, an archaic, dilapidated warehouse in the long since demised business district in my town, he continued using his cock as his main thinking head. I had to chuckle at this. Tanner was by far my easiest prey so far. I didn't even break a sweat!

"We're here, baby," I purred seductively to him in his ear. I threw up in my mouth a little doing so; he smelled like he had bathed in Tom Ford for fuck's sake!

"Damn, baby," Tanner slurred, "You live in a real shit hole."

"Well, good thing you aren't at fucking my *place*, sugar," I retorted with a wink. Tanner's stupid face lit up like a kid on Christmas morning. Jesus, men are just the worst, right? He followed behind me as I entered the facility, nipping at my heels like a lovesick puppy. I felt like a Black Widow spider watching my next meal edge closer and closer to my web and its inevitable demise. A rictus grin spread across my face as we approached the makeshift kitchen.

"How about another drink, hon," I purred in my best baby voice, you know the kind that guys eat up like a fully loaded pizza.

"You trying to get me drunk, Morticia?" Tanner teased.

"No way, sugar, I want you totally levelheaded so I can get some of that good dick!"

"That won't be a problem," Tanner mused. "Good dick is what I excel at!"

Fuck me gently with a chainsaw, I groaned to myself. I couldn't wait to get this fucker tied up so I can fuck him up. He oozed with so much arrogance and misogyny it was physically repellent. He was a literal #MeToo meme for fucks sake.

As I prepared his final drink ever, I crushed the olive-green Rohypnol pill into his cup and stirred it until the contents had fully dissolved. Handing him his drink, I smiled wickedly.

"Here's to a night you'll never forget," I exclaimed, as he chugged his drink in one gigantic gulp.

"Hell yeah, bitch," he slurred, "I'm going to knock those boots all the way to Albuquerque like Bugs Bunny!"

The fact that he gets so much pussy is truly a shocker to me; this cretin had zero game. I guess it goes to show how desperate or just plain idiotic most females truly are these days. I weep for my kind and how pathetic we can sometimes be.

"I can't wait to get my hands on you," I said. The double meaning going totally over the head of this Neanderthal.

"Me...either, babbbbyyyy," Tanner drunkenly slurred.

I could see the drugs were taking hold. Tanner began to stagger and fell heavily into the chair he was standing next to. His eyes rolled back into his numb skull, and he passed out nearly immediately, drool already flowing freely from his sagging, gaping mouth.

"It's Showtime, bubba," I mused to myself, and set to work getting him ready for his first, and last big screen debut.

\*\*\*

Tanner's slumber is rudely interrupted by a hellacious slap to his face that leaves a reddening imprint of my hand across his right cheek. His head rocks violently as he is expelled from his drug-induced siesta.

"Well, look who finally decided to join us, ladies and gentlemen," I laugh.

"What's going on here, why am I tied to this chair?"

"Shut up!" I roar at his bewildered, sleep puffy face. He stares at me, befuddled by the drastic and severe evolution that the night has suddenly taken.

"What's going on here, is that women are sick of your shit, and it is the end of the road for your pathetic, loser ass!"

Tanner looks at me with nothing but pure malice in his eyes, and by the looks of him he's getting ready to try and tell me off or threaten me somehow. So, before he can, I strike him as hard as I can manage right on the bridge of his nose, breaking it in two places. Blood flows freely down his face, resembling a broken water faucet, stunning him into silence before a single word can even be spoken.

"You just sit there and be a good boy, if you know what is good for you. Just kidding, do whatever the fuck you want, I'm still going to kill you!"

"Kill me?" Tanner moans, "Why? I never did anything to you."

"Maybe not to me personally, but you sure as fuck have abused countless women, and that shit stops tonight. We aren't just inanimate objects for you to play with, and then cast off after you've broken us like a willful, arrogant child."

I go to my desktop to check all the messages, and to no one's surprise whatsoever, everybody was thirsty for blood: Man blood. And so am I. I have Tanner set up in the middle of the room, tied to an old chair I found cast away at the local dump. He is surrounded by ring lights to make sure the ensuing carnage will be perfectly lit for all to enjoy. Directly in front of Tanner is a huge wicker basket filled with rocks of varying sizes and shapes. His eyes follow my hand as I sift through the stones searching for the perfect one to start tonight's festivities. I rub the rocks seductively like a lover might in the heat of lovemaking. I am already getting heavily aroused, and I haven't even hit him yet.

Tanner looks at me balefully, his fury throbbing from him like a living thing. His voice cracks as he violently spits a tirade out.

"So, you're going to kill me based off some dumb bitch running her dick sucker mouth about me? Because let me tell you, Rayne is just a drama queen cunt who is too fugly to get her own man, and furthermore what I do with Jamie is nobodies..."

That's as far as I let him get before I whizz the first stone directly at his vulgar, woman-hating mouth. The force sends most of his teeth shattering out of his bloody mouth like pins from a bowler's strike! The sound is oh so delicious to my ears, a true pop hit if I ever heard one!

Tanner has an utterly incredulous look on his face. I don't think he ever thought I was going to really hurt him. Obviously, the joke was on him. The rock is halfway hanging out of his mouth as he expels it along with a handful of teeth and a copious amount of blood when he forcefully vomits it all out onto his lap. The tough guy façade is now a mere shadow of its former self; Tanner is visually trembling and crying. It makes me infinitely wetter taking away his manhood like I just did. I feel very powerful, almost godlike.

"You don't have to do this," he screeches as he continues to weep.

"You taught me a lesson; I won't treat women like garbage anymore, I promise!"

"You're so full of shit, Tanner, that your eyes are brown, now, unless you have any final words, allow me to retort."

I see a flash of sardonic hate flash in his eyes, as Tanner tries to muster one last shot of machismo at me.

"You dirty cunt, I'm going to get loose and sodomize you with my fist ..." he hisses, his eyes full of hate.

But that is all that escapes his mouth before the next stone comes speeding at his left eye like a rocket. The impact makes a nauseating, thudding sound as the sharp end of the rock imbeds itself in Tanner's pupil, puncturing it with shocking ease. An animalistic sound emanates out of Tanner's ruined mouth as he shakes his head back and forth, trying desperately to dislodge the stone. The moment he stops, I lob the next rock directly at his already damaged eye, lodging it further into his optic cavity.

"Looks like you're the one getting penetrated tonight," I giggle. "I hope I'm not too big for you, baby!"

Tanner is locked in a silent scream; no sound radiates from his throat. It is obvious that I broke his eye socket, and most of the bones surrounding his ocular cavity, with the second hurl. Blood and optic fluid cascades down his cheek as he struggles in vain against his shackles. Even with the rock embedded in his eye, you can see the massive swelling and discoloration of his face surrounding it. Veins protrude visibly from his forehead as if he was straining to lift an impossibly heavy weight.

"Please stop!" he wails, but I am only getting warmed up for the bastard.

I walk up and pluck the stone from his socket, taking most of his damaged eye with me as I extract it. I feel a slight tug and look down to see what the holdup is. That's when I see that his optic nerve is still tethered inside of his worthless skull. Wordlessly shrugging to myself, I go to my work desk and pick up a large pair of shears. For dramatic effect, I snip them close to his nose, scaring Tanner, and causing his one good eye to bulge out cartoonishly in fear. He lets out a torrent of piss as he cries and hysterically mumbles to himself.

"Dammit, Tanner, you could have at least warned me you were going to piss yourself like a mongrel so I could have at least put down some newspapers," I snarl.

With shears in hand, I pull the ropy stalks of his sockets nice and taut as I snip them loose with my shears, playfully slapping Tanner's face with his newly excommunicated eyeball. A fresh jet of blood flows down his face like he has just witnessed the saddest thing imaginable. I lovingly lap up the blood and tongue his newly made orifice deep and with fervor. After my tongue snakes out of his yawning eye socket, it is covered in all sorts of meaty, bloody goodness, so I hungrily swallow it right up. I smack my lips in appreciation, sauntering back to my rock pile and begin flinging the stones at Tanner with perfect precision. They hit him in his chest, shoulder, knees and groin in a rapid succession like I am the Nolan Ryan of rock pelting. Tanner's panting cries become more incessant and pathetic as the numerous stones take their toll on his freshly decimated form.

"Momma, I want my momma," Tanner moans in pure agony.

"You want your precious Mommy, little baby?"

"Yes", he whispers almost inaudibly.

"Let me tell you something about your momma," I snicker.

"If that worthless cunt was here right now, I would literally stuff her heinous, smelly cooze full of these rocks right here, and drop that bitch in the river to drown, just for having a worthless son like you!"

From the nonstop pinging of IM's, and the Cha-Ching sound of everyone tipping me in my preferred method of payment, Crypto Currency, I can tell it is going to be a great night in terms of bodily destruction AND a lucrative payday! It's time for the grand finale to begin.

I mug for my fans by getting behind Tanner and simultaneously hugging him and kissing his blood covered cheek. I also throw up a peace sign like every other E-Girl thot on the internet seems to do these days. I feel like a blood-caked Belle Delphine, but I digress. I do that a lot, don't I?

"It's time for ole Tanner boy to cease being a member of the living, but since I'm such a compassionate and caring host, I thought I'd let you have some parting words to the audience before I crush your head into smithereens with that final stone over there, like Gallagher with a watermelon."

Tanner's head lolls around like his neck is almost too weak to support it. He glances at me briefly with malevolence in his eyes before he looks directly at the camera.

"Mom, Dad, and Kim, I love you guys with all my heart. I'll miss you, so much. I'm sorry I wasn't a better son and brother while I had the chance."

"Wait a minute," I say incredulously, "Is your last name White?"

"Yes."

"Well, just like that annoying song, isn't this a very small fucking world after all?" I guffaw.

"Kim White was the biggest bitch to me in high school, she's the epitome of a true cunt, and was my biggest nemesis. That worthless excuse for a human being made my life miserable. It feels truly wonderful to know I'm killing someone she loves."

I head to the basket and retrieve the final stone. I give it a kiss and look at Tanner with all the emotion of someone seeing roadkill on the road. I feel absolutely nothing.

I place the rock into my dominant left hand and raise it above my head as I look deeply into my Tanner's remaining eye. He stares back at me as well, unblinking, resigned to the fact that he is about to die. He says nothing and neither do I. I bring the rock down with all the force I can muster, while letting out a guttural howl like an unhinged creature. The stone makes a truly satisfying "*TWAK*" sound as it crashes into his forehead. The skin separates from itself, showing the white gleam of his skull before the blood begins to spill down his face by the gallon.

I strike the same spot again, and this time, I'm rewarded with the loud cracking sound of his skull breaking in half. Actual fragments of bone fly out from the sheer force of my brutal assault. Without the protection of his skull to hold everything in place, I am fascinated to see his brain matter slowly pour out of his forehead like a child with a snot-caked, runny nose. I hammer down blows upon his stupid face, fracturing both cheek bones, not to mention caving in his other orbital lobe, and swelling his lone eye shut to almost ridiculous levels. His misshapen head begins to take on the color of a ripe eggplant from all the damage I am dishing out.

The more I pound his head, the more I can tell that his skull is turning to literal dust. I watch as his noggin becomes reminiscent of a burlap sack falling over and spilling its contents onto the floor haphazardly. I savagely strike his mouth with the sharp end of the stone, sending his last remaining teeth clattering in every direction, and making his mouth look like a cavernous, bloody hole. His plasma-coated, brain-covered tongue hangs out of his mouth obscenely as a deluge of blood pours down his face like the scene in Carrie. His mouth is making these quick gasping breaths as his body starts to spasm uncontrollably. He is obviously in his death throes. He is making these gross sounding gurgles, letting me know he is making his death rattle. He is dying, and I never felt more fucking alive! Almost as an afterthought, I grab a small paring knife and cut loose his drooping tongue in three quick, efficient hacks.

"I think I'll pleasure my throbbing pussy with this afterwards, then leave it outside in the elements so it can get nice and putrefied, and maggot-riddled for even more pleasure for myself at a later date."

Even though Tanner is clearly dead now, I still want to commit one last atrocity to him, for the fans, of course. On the ground, I have a bunch of cinder blocks laying carelessly about, and inspiration hits me like a ton of bricks, pun very much intended!

With a small grunt, I lift the block with both hands and crash it down on Tanner's damaged head. The little bit of strength that his skull has is no match for the ferocity of my blow, and his entire head explodes like the infamous Scanners scene, belching forth a geyser of gore onto me in the process, coating me in skull fragments, brain matter, flecks of dead skin and God knows what else. I am coated from head to toe! I need a shower and I really need to please my pulsating pussy with that severed tongue! Feeling that I kicked mucho ass for tonight's livestream, I look at the camera, preparing to speak.

"Alright guys, I hope you enjoyed the show, let's have a round of applause for our guest of dishonor, Tanner. I mean, I like getting stoned sometimes too, but this is ridiculous!"

I wink to the camera and blow a kiss to all my fans. I feel like I'm on top of the world. Killing some douche bag always gives me such an amazing high, nothing comes close to it. Nothing can ruin this night...well, that's what I think as I log off the computer and head towards the shower. Turns out shit is going to take a turn for the worse way sooner than later...

*Since episode one, it is time to watch tonight's lurid livestream from my revolting Redroom! Sorry, I was channeling my inner Crypt Keeper! XOXOXO!*

# Chapter Two

---

# An Offer I Couldn't Refuse

After I rub one out with the help of Tanner's freshly detached tongue, and take a long, hot shower, I head into the kitchen to get myself a nightcap and to check a few emails before going to bed. My body is sore as fuck from all the exertion I just put myself through. Beating someone to death with rocks is like the best workout ever, trust me! As I browse the myriad of emails cluttering up my inbox, I notice one that is pure bait material. It simply says "READ ME OR ELSE!"

This email is really grating my nerves because it is the fifth time it showed up in my inbox. I normally just delete the damn thing, but I'm feeling good, so I think I will fuck with them. I figure it is a horny fan trying to get my attention or something lame like that. I am Jack's mild annoyance.

I open the email, and it only has a number for me to call with the cryptic message, *Make the call, it's the difference between life and death!*

"Well, mysterious emailer, you had my curiosity, but now you have my attention!" I muse aloud with a hearty laugh.

And just like that, I dial the number. It rings exactly four times before it is picked up. I can't even get a word in before the voice on the other end abruptly begins to speak.

"I'm glad you finally had the good sense to call and not make this any more difficult than it needs to be."

"Well, I do like to make things difficult, but you caught me after a particularly amazing night of pure debauchery and mayhem, and I'd like nothing more than to go to bed, so, let's cut the chit chat. Why do you keep bugging me, loser?"

"You must be tired from brutally killing that young man tonight, I'm sure."

Now, that statement gives me pause. This fucker doesn't even remotely sound like a fan. As a matter of fact, just his voice alone is giving me the creeps and I have nerves of fucking steel.

"Look, Dipshit, say what you have to say because I'm about two seconds from hanging the fuck up on your creepy ass!"

The phone is silent for a nanosecond before he brusquely replies.

"Listen to me, Morticia, like your life depends on it, and believe me, it does. I'm going to give you something that I didn't give your rival, Simon, a choice.

You see, unbeknownst to you or that shithead Simon, there's only room in town for one major snuff film production company and that's us. Hurt 2 The Core to be exact."

"So, let me guess," I sass, "If I don't stop, you're going to run me out of town, right?"

"Not quite. You have something that we want or otherwise you would be dead like Simon."

I freeze; did he just say dead?

"Hello?" the voice says.

"I'm here," I retort.

"Good to see I have your total attention now."

At that moment, a picture of Simon pops up on my laptop. It looks as if he has been shot repeatedly in the head and chest with a very large caliber pistol. The entire left quadrant of his head is totally gone. He has bullet holes going through both cheeks, and each eye has been shot point blank, leaving grisly, gore-filled holes to emptily stare back at me from the picture. I silently gulp in fear. These fuckers have my full attention, that's for sure.

"Like I said, luckily, you have something special going for you. You have a rabid fan base, and you only kill men; that's something we don't have a market for on here yet at H2TC.com."

"Simon was just a roach that needed to be squashed out of existence, but you, you're special."

"Aww, I bet you say that to all the girls, bub," I say in mock disdain.

"The name is Lux. Now, when you come on board with us, your site goes black, understand?"

"I haven't decided just..."

"Quit acting like a petulant little brat, you have nothing to decide. You either come work for me, and my people, or you will be dead by dawn!"

"Well, when you put it like that, Luxie, how can a girl refuse?"

"Look, this is a prime gig. You will have you very own warehouse, with a fully loaded Redroom on the Dark Web, filled with all the implements you could ever desire to butcher a human being. You will still be permitted to snuff out males exclusively as you are accustomed to, and you'll never have to worry about getting caught by the authorities, as they are all paid off rather handsomely. Plus, you'll have two other helpers to do the other films that are, how should I say this, unsavory. The kind of films our more wicked and depraved buyer's request."

"Sorry, Luxie, but I'm a solo act, I don't need help."

"You're getting help and that's it. One guy to fuck and kill the females and one guy to fuck and kill the babies and children."

"Babies and kids? What the fuck, dude!" I was horrified by that, but not really surprised, the world is ruled by sickos.

"Use your head, woman," Lux fumes.

"You think there's only people who are content with men and women raped and murdered? Hell, CP is our bread and butter here. Daisy's Destruction alone netted us over six figures last year.  But like I said earlier," Lux continues,

"You will not have to sully yourself with these things. As a matter of fact, you don't even have to fraternize with either gentleman, if that is your prerogative."

There is no point in trying to fight this right now. I am backed against a wall and Lux knows it. He holds all the cards, the smug, arrogant bastard. I will enjoy ripping his throat out with my teeth one day. I just have to chill and play the role of hapless female until I can figure out what to do. Let him think he's got me beat; that shit will be his downfall, and I'll make him suffer like he has never dreamed of!

"So, when do I go to the compound?"

"A car is on the way to your residence as we speak."

"Let me guess, your driver will blindfold me and take me to a secret location."

"As a matter of fact, you are one hundred percent correct."

I am Jack's utter contempt and exasperation.

"Well, let's get this shit show on the road," I say coldly.

"The car is on the way, Morticia, I suggest you get your belongings gathered. My driver will text you once he has arrived at your domicile."

"Yippee," I say in my bitchiest tone and hang up my phone.

I chew my lip as I stare at my room and try to figure out which of my belongings I'm going to take as a defense mechanism to deflect from the fact that I'm basically being kidnapped against my will.

Even though my blood is boiling, there's a small part of me that is somewhat jubilant about this predicament I've landed myself into. If anything, my life is never boring, that is for sure.

I start packing my meager belongings and prepare for a new chapter in my crazy so-called life.

# Chapter Three

# Lux

Lux hangs up the phone, and rewatches Morticia's latest snuff livestream. He has to give it to the snarky, arrogant bitch. Her shows always bring inventive and original killing ideas. She also has a huge fan base, the one fact that kept her from ending up like Simon's unoriginal ass. He wants her dead as well because he knows she is going to be a major thorn in his side for the duration of this new "partnership." She's young, brash, and above all else, utterly insane, a bad combination any way you look at it.

Lux was informed by *his* boss, as well as the higher ups in the company, that numerous high-roller customers clamored for films done exclusively by Morticia almost daily. Lux pled his case against recruiting her vehemently but was immediately outvoted. This, of course, left a bad taste in his mouth that still hasn't dissipated. He already disliked the girl just on principal alone, but the decision was never his to make, and there is nothing left to do but suck it up and get on board.

He is certainly not going to make waves and end up with a bullet in his head, or worse, get a starring role in one of the many upcoming snuff films. Knowing his luck, they'd probably give the job to Morticia too. He knows she will come up with something extremely vile and repugnant way to extinguish his flame. Nope, Lux will play ball for now. He made sure to record her latest livestream though. Something in his gut tells him he might need that footage one day, and he always listens to his gut.

# Chapter Four

---

# The Three Amigos

Just like Lux said, a driver did indeed come pick me up at my place, and the prick also made me put on a fucking handkerchief for "security reasons." These mother fuckers watch way too many movies! I called bullshit in my head, but since I am playing the good, obedient girl for the moment, I'm not going to rock the boat just yet. I am Jack's total cooperation. As I ride in utter silence to my new home, I lament on how quickly life can take a giant shit on your lap sometimes. Earlier, I was crushing a predator's head with a football sized stone with not a care in the world, and now I've got to play ball with these shady fucks or end up literal worm food.

Fuck the male patriarchy, I tell you! I try to get this miserable motherfucker driving to indulge me with some idle chit chat, but of course, he is as mute as Helen Keller, but without the talent. So, with an audible sigh, I just sit back and wait to see what my new digs will be like in the silence of the night. As the car comes to a stop, my door is opened, and I'm being helped from the car by rough, callused hands as my blindfold is yanked off.

I blink momentarily, blinded by the sudden brightness. We've pulled into the actual building, so I have no way of using any landmarks to hopefully try and figure where I've been taken. Great, another fucking L for myself. I look to my driver to explain what the next step will be, but to my chagrin he is furiously typing out a text and paying me absolutely no mind whatsoever.

"So, uh, what's next?" I venture to the oblivious, prick driver.

"I'm letting Lurch know you're here," the driver says with a huff.

"Lurch? Are we on the set of a new Addams Family movie or something?" I jokingly inquire. Literal crickets meet my unanswered banter. I bet this guy is a real blast at parties: Not! If I get the chance, I hope to gut this turd like a fish one day and do the Twist like Chubby Checker in his freshly spilled innards. After an awkward silence, the oblivious prick driver spouts, "Lurch will show you the ropes and take you to your sector. He works here too. He takes care of the films that feature women. Pat Bale handles the CP and the crazier, psychotic requests. You'll see him later after he finishes filming."

"Ok, when do I meet with Lux though?"

"You'll never actually meet him in person. You'll converse with him either by text or FaceTime.

Now if you will excuse me, my shift is over, and I'm going home. Like I said, Lurch should be up in a moment to show you the lay of the land."

And with that he quickly strides to an elevator that requires a thumbprint and keycard and presses the button for the first floor. We are on the basement level presently, it seems. I wonder what crazy ass company would be cool with real Redroom's butchering people right below their feet and figured I don't want to know. Behind me, I hear a door closing and turn towards the sound, expecting to finally meet Lurch. I figure he will be exceptionally tall as his name suggests. What I don't expect, however, is to be face to face with a genuine monster. An audible yelp escapes my throat before I can catch it, as I stare at the behemoth walking directly towards me. His height is extreme, the entryway is easily six feet tall, and he still has to stoop to walk through it.

He is as wide as two full grown men walking side by side, but he is not fat; far from it. As a matter of fact, he is muscular beyond belief, the closest thing I've seen to someone realistically resembling The Incredible Hulk. His vascularity is through the roof, making even the most hardened bodybuilder look miniscule in comparison. He looks like he could rip a human being in half with just his bare hands. But the most terrifying thing about him is his head. He suffers from a malady called Megacephalous, which means he has an abnormally large head. One of his eyes are the size of a grapefruit and the other looks to be non-functioning and the size of a large grape.

He smiles at me like a lunatic as he gets closer and reveals teeth that wouldn't seem out of place inside a shark's gaping maw. He is wearing an archaic pair of Key brand bib overalls that seem to be straining to stay attached to his hulking form, and he smells bad enough to knock a sea of flies off a shit and corpse filled wagon. He also appears to be covered in blood, semen and God knows what else, with an underlying stench of excrement to boot. And just like that he is upon me and reaching out for my trembling form. I feel like Han Solo, frozen in carbonite, unable to defend myself due to the shock. He grabs me with both arms and pulls me in for a bear hug! In a comical voice that doesn't remotely resemble his inhuman visage, he says heartily,

"Howdy, Miss Morticia, the name is Lurch and I'm pleased ta meet ya!"

"Uh, hey, Lurch. Nice to meet you too," I say, totally flummoxed.

I feel like I am in some crazy movie, not real life. Everything has a vague, dreamlike feeling that I can't shake off no matter how hard I try...

"Want some tittymeat?"

"Huh?"

"Tittymeat," Lurch says again. "I like to put it in my mouth and use it like 'backer and chew on it!"

He is literally chewing on the remnants of a dead woman's ripped off breast like it is a wad of chewing tobacco. Even for me that's a new one.

"Uh, maybe later," I say.

"It's been a very long day and I just want to find my room and go to bed."

"I hear ya, I tells yuh what, as we head towards your room, imma give you a nice lil' tour, okay, Miss Morticia?"

He looks at me with big - well one, at least - expectant eyes. He strikes me as very lonely, and I feel a quick kinship manifest itself once the shock dissipates. I look at the big goon, smile, and say, "Sure, Lurch, lead the way!"

As we traverse the underground compound, I silently listen as Lurch excitedly talks about this and that. He shows me our quarters, the gym, an expansive pool, and the cafeteria. I grip his massive shoulder which causes him to stop talking and look down at me.

"So, are you telling me we can't leave the compound, Lurch?"

"Well, I's never gets to leave here, Miss Morticia, and I heard from security that the same thing goes for you, I's afraid."

I look at Lurch miserably and shake my head slowly.

"What about Pat Bale? Does he get to leave?"

"Yessum, he can come and go since he's the star here. Lux said his movies make the most money by far."

"And what kind of movies does he make, Lurch?" I already know, but I'm curious what the giant man would tell me.

"Oh, he makes the nasty ones, Miss Morticia! The ones where he tortures women folk 'til they suffer for hours on end before they's kick the bucket, and all the kiddie videos. He rapes and kills 'em too. He is a bad man, Miss Morticia, he scares me!"

I watch in shock as this monster of a man shivers uncontrollably, and a big, lone teardrop plummets from his one good eye and drops to the ground. I gently massage his back and hush him until he straightens up and sucks up his snot trail from his nose, chews on it a bit, and spits the yellow, brown, and red concoction out of his mouth like a shotgun. It splatters against the far wall and begins its slow descent, sliding down, leaving a hideous trail in its wake.

"How's about we go check out your Redroom's now?"

"Lead the way, big boy, I'm anxious to get my hands dirty, to be honest. That cocksucker Lux has me in a bind and I need to kill me a man ASAP!"

Lurch visibly gulps at that comment and warily looks at me with that grapefruit sized, crazy eye of his darting around. It would almost be comical and pathetic if I wasn't on the verge of loving the big, kindhearted idiot already.

"Lurch, can I ask you something?

"Uh huh."

"Do you like killing people?"

"No, ma'am, not anymore. When I was a youngin' maybe. But they mostly died because I didn't know my own strength. Oh, and my pecker of course."

"That takes the term of fucking someone to death to a whole new level, bubba!"

I begin to giggle as I playfully punch his arm, which causes Lurch to blush and laugh as well.

"Tomorrow, I's got me a picture to film, so you're more than welcome to watch. We have bulletproofed, two-way mirrors that Lux or whoever can watch us making our flicks if they want to."

"Does that happen often?"

Lurch ponders this for a second, then replies,

"Sometimes when big wigs from out of town want to see the action up close and personal, then yessum, mostly it's Lux though."

"Well maybe I can wring his scrawny ne…"

Lurch immediately slaps his big, sweaty palm around my face before I can finish my sentence.

"Shush, Miss Morticia, they's gots all sorts of cameras and listening devices in here. Don't need you threatenin' the boss and getting' yerself in trouble or even kilt!"

It has been a very long time since I cared for anyone but myself, so imagine how perplexed I felt knowing that this monstrosity immediately became like my BFF. Too bad I don't have a necklace to split with him, right?

"Thanks, bubba, guess I got a lot to learn about this place, huh?"

As we approach the three soundproofed doors that are our killing rooms, one of them opens, revealing a gore covered, nude man, strutting out whistling "Hip to Be Square" by Huey Lewis and The News. His erection juts out in front of him, like a pregnant woman's bulbous belly, equally blood covered. He looks almost euphoric from whatever business he was up to in there, and judging from his visage, it must have been a massacre. He looks exactly like that scene in American Psycho where the nude killer came out with a chainsaw, chasing after the prostitute to saw her up into pieces. Minus the saw, of course, duh!

"Ah, you must be our first official man killer! The name is Pat Bale, put er there."

And with that, he takes my hand and gives me the most painful handshake of my life. It is like my hand was put into a vice and was being squashed. He grins maniacally as he sees the pain on my face. He has the eyes of a Great White shark, the onyx optics emitting no emotion as it takes a giant chunk out of you. They are the blackest eyes, the Devil's eyes. I look to Lurch, and he looks mad as hell, but equally scared as shit. It is up to me to call this sociopath's bluff. With all my strength, I squeeze back as I look straight into his eyes and force myself to match his smile tit for tat.

For a moment he gives nothing away, but I am determined not to let a man terrify me like he's trying to do right now. I persevere and give him a grin right back that would make the Cheshire Cat jealous AF. Pat's grin falters just a little, wilting at the corners ever so slightly. It's only noticeable if you are looking specifically for it. Small, yes, but it is there. It lets him know that he can take his toxic masculinity and stick it right up his yuppie asshole.

Our silent showdown for the time being was on hold, both of us bent somewhat, but neither broke entirely. I will have to keep my eye on this bastard though. I watch as he surveys my curves like a man choosing a new car and grimace in disgust as he visually licks his lips like some fucking Tex Avery cartoon wolf.

"Has the mongoloid given you a decent tour of the compound? I'd be pleased as punch to take you around myself, after I get all this delicious infant blood off me, I still need to finish playing with her, of course. She has not suffered nearly enough."

He has that smug, better than you, grin back on his chiseled, perfect face. Yeah, I'll give it to the creep, he looks like a GQ model I suppose, but otherwise he is just a piece of shit baby rapist to me.

"Nope, Lurch did perfectly fine with the tour and introductions. I doubt you could top him."

I can tell from the pained squint in his eyes that I offended him. Good! Maybe I can knock this pompous prick down a peg or two while I'm here.

"Well, then," Pat begins, "I'll let you two get back to it. This baby isn't going to fuck and mutilate herself."

And with that he strides to his door and opens it, giving me a brief glimpse of a female toddler strapped to a gurney. She is nude and her face is almost plum in color from crying incessantly. I can see that almost her entire right leg's skin is flayed off. Thankfully the door closes as quickly as it opened, shielding me from the atrocities inside.

"Sorry, Miss Morticia," Lurch bemoans.

"I'm awfully afraid of him, he is meaner than a wicker basket full of cobras, he is. He picks on me every chance he gets."

"Well, Lurch," I say, "You got me now and he isn't going to bother you ever again, okay?"

"Okay!"

"Now, let's finish the tour, shall we?"

"Yes, ma'am!"

# Chapter Five

# Kim White Gets Answers

Fuck, I wish I could kill Tanner sometimes, no scratch that, I'd say most times. Here I am, or was, in New York City doing a month-long Gucci modeling shoot that I have to cut short on account of his worthless ass dropping off the face of the planet. I can't even get him to at least text me back, but last week when he needed money he had the quickest texting hands in the fucking west, let me tell you. And what was he doing with all the money I was sending back home to him?

By the looks of this derelict motel he is squatting in, it is probably going straight up his nostrils. So, maybe he is on a drug bender, but he usually stays in touch with me, dammit. That's why I had to come check on his underachieving ass. He has been my cross to bear since our parent's died in a mysterious – well, not to me - car crash and the family fortune went to the both of us. I, of course, being the trustee since Tanner would have bought a Bugatti for every day of the week. Spoiled is an understatement of the century when it comes to my baby brother.

He was always very weak and testy, leaving me to clean up messes, especially female trouble messes. He can go from simp to abuser in an instant. It probably would be better to kill the bastard, but blood is blood, and he is all I have left. In a way, he is one of the last vestiges of my waning humanity.

\*\*\*

I arrive at the Admiral Motel and am greeted by the epitome of seedy. It's almost like he sought out the most clichéd, shit hole in the entire city to take up residence. The smell of weed tinged with desperation permeates the air as I step out of the taxi and pay the driver. As I stride towards the Manager's office, I notice some security cameras along the perimeter. I pray they work even though I don't want to be identified coming here. The hoodie and the Audrey Hepburn, Breakfast at Tiffany's glasses should do the trick, I imagine. I arrive at the apartment manager's door and brusquely stride inside to the hideous sight of a fat, sweaty, and extremely hairy ass staring me right in the face. Its owner is breathing like a racehorse making its final lap to victory, as he desperately tries to plug in a DeWalt pneumatic nail gun.

"FUCK!" he wails pathetically to himself.

"Go into your hole, you worthless whore!"

Biting a contorted grin, I clear my throat loudly, causing the man to freeze into place.

"Pardon me, but are you the proprietor of this fine establishment?" I ask demurely.

He audibly groans and stands bolt upright faster than I would have guessed. Numerous bones pop in a pained rebuttal from his expenditure of exertion.

"Why, yes, I am, ma'am. The name is Felix. What can I do for you?"

He shakes my hand, and I am immediately repulsed by his cold, clammy touch. Rivulets of sweat cascades down his brow as he clears his throat and looks at me in equal measures of timidity and exasperation. Clearly, he is not a people person, which is fine by me. Humanity has long abandoned me like a fickle lover, but I can still fake it with the best of them, so I give him my million-dollar smile and that seems to calm him down to a degree.

"Well, Felix, I was hoping you could help me find out where my brother was last seen or who last saw him. I saw the security cameras and was hoping to get a look at them? His name is Tanner White."

"Hmm, well, the name doesn't ring a bell, but most people that use this establishment, how should I put it, want to stay under the radar, if you get my meaning. Hell, most only pay in cash. Don't ask, don't tell, type of mentality between them and I."

"Yes, I certainly can appreciate that, Felix, and I hate to be a pest, but he is a fragile young man and I need to know that he is alright, you understand that, don't you?"

"I certainly can, ma'am, but you see, that sounds an awful lot like a you type of problem, not mine. I find it best to stay out of the business of my patrons, so if you don't mind, I'd like to get back to some repairs I need to attend to. Good night."

And with that the corpulent fuck turns around and goes back to unsuccessfully trying to plug in the DeWalt nail gun, dismissing me like a class at the end of a humid school day. Good, I really want to do this the hard way. I silently slide my hands into my pockets, procure my gloves, and quickly put them on effortlessly, as I walk closer to where Felix, the human ass crack, is desperately trying to plug in the apparatus to no avail. I get the feeling that is how he has ventured through his fifty some odd years, just clumsily trying to eke out an existence without much success.

But today, Felix made the mistake of kicking the hornets' nest and he is going to get stung. With all my ample force, I kick him as hard as I can in that fat ass of his, sending him slamming face first into the wall, cracking the plaster and sheetrock. A kind of ridiculous wail emits from his bloodied mouth, as he shakes the drywall dust off his shocked face. I must admit, a weak, and vulnerable man kind of gets my engine revving, if you follow my drift.

"Listen up, asshole," I command. He stares at me and shivers like someone trapped outside during a hellacious blizzard.

"I realize I look like Paris Hilton in her prime, but I'll let you in on a little secret, ok? Did you know that I'm utterly insane and I have a bloodlust the size of Dahmer, Gacy, and Bundy combined? Of course not, you judged me as little more than a nuisance, I was distracting you from the incredibly hard job of plugging something into an outlet. Well, allow me to help you out, Felix, I insist."

As I go to do just that, he miraculously finds the hole, plunges it in, and flips to his back in a nano second, surprising both me and him with his speed.

"Fuck you, you crazy bitch!"

A rapid succession of tenpenny nails hit me in the arm and shoulder before I can knock the gun from his feeble grip. My lack of concern or emotion towards my wounds wipe off that momentary look of victory that seemed so foreign on his ugly face. It was almost comical watching that tiny shred of hope evaporate from his ugly mug, like the remnants of a rainstorm once the sun comes back out.

"Felix, I'm going to let you in on two little secrets about me. The first is I have a medical condition called CIPA which stands for congenital insensitivity to pain and anhidrosis. In simple terms, it means I'm incapable of feeling pain. Incidentally, it makes me unable to sweat but that's neither here nor there."

"What's the second secret?" Felix queried.

"Well, the second secret is I'm a serial killer, and I'm fucking good at it. Originally, I was just going to sweet talk you or flirt with you until you let me peruse the video footage of my brother's room. Now, though, I'm going to torture and kill you, and I'm still going to look through the files anyway, so it's definitely a win-win situation for me."

I drag Felix's worthless ass to his chair and fling him into it, watching him thud heavily into the seat with a cry of protest that wholly disgusts me. I grab the nail gun and shoot sixteen nails in both of his arms, trapping him to his chair. Just for safe measure, I do the same to both of his legs. His cries of pain bring immense pleasure to me. I glance around his office until my eyes set sight on an old leather tool bag cast into the corner like an unwanted thought.

I pilfer through its contents until I find the two items I was hoping were in there. I watch Felix's eyes enlarge to comical levels. What two items did I pull out, you might wonder? Well, I'll tell you. A nine-inch flathead screwdriver and an old claw hammer, probably as archaic as he is.

"What are you going to do with those things?"

"Well, Felix, I'm going to take this screwdriver, place it directly in the slit of your dick hole and use this hammer to drive it all the way down into your urethra. I'll probably beat your testicles with the hammer just for fun. Are you ready?"

I wrench his pants and underwear down in one swift pull, surprising us both like a magician with a particularly good parlor trick.

I watch all the blood drain from his face as he feels the unyielding steel penetrate the tip of his penis. Felix takes a deep breath and begins to open his mouth to blubber some sort of mixture of words to get me to stop, but I just put my fingertips to his lips and wordlessly mouth "Shush."

I raise the hammer before his synapses can even fire the information to his brain. I drive the hammer down with full force directly on the head of the screwdriver, sending it five inches deep into his urethra. His penis bulges grotesquely as the tool digs its way into his shaft. I continue to pound the hammer and manipulate the weapon even further, with gusto, and watch in fascination as the steel disappears completely into his penis, leaving only the handle exposed. Felix howls in agony as he tries to move his appendages to absolutely no avail. He's screaming and pleading something to me, and even though I'm there in front of him, it's only in a physical sense. My mind is, I don't know, elsewhere, fixated on the darkness, always the darkness.

After my fugue state dissipates, the volume of reality gets turned back up to a normal decibel, and Felix is trembling and moaning for his mother. I blanche at his worthless vis-age and begin slowly pulling the screwdriver from his ruined urethra and mangled ejaculatory duct. Gore-streaked steel slowly begins to appear from his cock, as well as an ample amount of blood. Its oil-like consistency impedes the process exponentially. With one final tug, the head of the tool erupts from his ruined cock, pieces of his prostate still attached to the flat headed device. His ruined penis spurts thick ropes of blood, mimicking semen. A final act of defiance to my destruction of his pathetic manhood.

"Just kill me," Felix says in a dry whisper that is barely audible.

"All in good time, let's see how long your adrenaline can keep you going."

"Please," Felix meekly begins just as I grasp the hammer and bring it down on his left testicle. The old hammer does its job very well. I watch in glee as his scrotum rips wide open from the force of my strike. Blood intermingled with shredded testicle meat steadily drips and pools onto the floor. His face becomes very ashen; he angles his head slightly to the side and vomits all over himself, passing out from the excruciating pain. Laughing to myself, I smash his final gonad with ferocious zeal. Felix didn't even move a muscle. Well,

I certainly can't have that. I carry smelling salts for this very reason; no way am I letting him miss out on all the fun for what is left of his worthless life. Amazingly, Felix lasts for another thirty minutes, not too shabby for an old timer.

*\*\*\**

After eviscerating and decapitating Felix, I take on the arduous task of combing through his surveillance footage and begin to chain smoke. Felix's head rests on the table beside me and I use his eyeless sockets to tap my ashes into like an ashtray. After I take the last drag, I extinguish my cigarette on his pallid tongue, which hangs out of his mouth like a spent penis after sex. His mouth is almost entirely filled up with cigarette butts, puffing out his cheeks like a squirrel gathering nuts. I scan the video files with a fine-tooth comb watching my brother's comings and goings. His Door Dash deliveries as well as his plug's drug deliveries. I finally hit pay dirt nearly two hours later when the countenance of the person responsible for my brother's death is finally revealed to me.

I stare at the screen in disbelief as anger begins to coarse through me like a ravenous infection. It's that disgusting cooze I used to humiliate in high school, Morticia Maggot. Her name, even inside my head, is like fingernails on chalkboards. I made it my mission in school to treat her no differently than the dog shit on the heel of my Prada slingback pumps. Something that needed to be cleaned up and thrown away. So, what was this then?

Some sort of revenge on my past sins against her gothic, trashy ass? If only I had started killing back then instead of taking out my murderous impulses on animals, my brother would still be here, and this whore would be nothing but a pile of moldering bones disintegrating in a shallow grave somewhere. Well, guess what, cunt? I'm coming for you, enjoy your life, what little there is of it left!

# Chapter Six

# Pat Bale Is A Cunt

It seems cliché as fuck, but time really does fly! It's been a little over a month that I've been at the compound making snuff flicks for Lux. I'm still a prisoner in terms of being able to leave, but otherwise, I'm free to roam the entire lower level, peruse the internet, and buy whatever I want. I'm being paid in cryptocurrency, and it is not regulated so I often go on buying sprees. Mostly books, kindle titles, and digital goregrind albums on Bandcamp. Lux says I will be granted the ability to leave soon, if I keep being a good girl. What a creepy thing to say to a woman, but what do you expect from a person that has no qualms having a man fist fuck a tween girl with no lube for the masturbatory delight of some sick fuck with the money to burn in front of you?

But today those dark thoughts aren't touching me. I'm having lunch with Lurch and I'm feeling optimistic about my situation. I am Jack's hopeful desires. It's funny how I have come to adore Lurch. Even though he looks like something out of a nightmare, he has been nothing but loving and protective of me. Everything would be okay if that sickening prick Pat wasn't around to poison the atmosphere with his fucking toxic masculinity. I try to always keep him in sight, out of the corner of my eye. He is always watching me, licking his lips, and repositioning his obvious erection. God knows what horrific shit he is imagining in his rape and murder fantasies of me.

Lurch sticks close to me, but the lovable behemoth fears him also. His terror blinds him to the fact that he could probably crush Pat with his bare hands. I guess it proves the difference between the two; one does bad things for a job, and one is just a bad person period. We are all killers that enjoy our work, to be sure, but Lurch and I have a "turnoff valve", if you will. Pat is the murderous, American psycho that he is all day, every day. He just has this presence that is so uncomfortable, and to be quite honest, uber scary. It's like having a feral wolf in your house pacing around. You know something awful is going to happen, you just don't know fucking when, and it is truly exhausting, if I'm being totally frank.

But as of late, dickface has been on vacation to the Hamptons, so it has just been Lurch and I. It has been an utter joy, let me tell you!

\*\*\*

It is lunchtime, so me and my mutant buddy are enjoying some excellent lasagna brought in by Little Italy, a terrific Italian restaurant we both love. After we have eaten our fill of the delectable grub, Lurch begins laboriously working on a drawing of his plan for the afternoon video that's been assigned to him. The crude drawing would be almost cute if I hadn't talked to him about it at length earlier and knew his plans for his hapless victim. Lurch looks almost comical with his tongue out and he has a look of total seriousness as he works on his drawing. Finally, with an audible sigh, he tosses down his crayons and looks at me with a smile.

"Drawings done, Miss Morticia!"

"Looks good, buddy, I would hate to be her."

"Yeah, this is gonna be a messy one fer sure. Gotta make the buyers happy, right?"

"Yeah, we wouldn't want to let the scummy, rich bastards down," I say with a wry smile and a gentle punch to Lurch's massive bicep.

"Isn't it great that Mr. Bale has been gone and it has jus' been us?"

"I couldn't agree more, Lurch, he could fuck up a wet dream!"

"Yup, he makes my belly ache with him callin' me stupid and always makin' googly eyes atcha."

"You've seen that, huh?" I ask.

"Yup, like he's havin' sex wit yuh with his eyes or somethin'."

"Yeah, well, don't worry your pretty little head bubba, I'm a big girl and can handle myself." I mock pose like I'm a WWE wrestler, causing Lurch to chuckle. His face becomes serious right after, then he speaks again.

"I's never forgive muhself if he hurt cha."

I kiss him on his unbelievably giant forehead and pat his shoulder.

"Lurch, my boy, nobody hurts me, I do the hurting!"

"Yessum!"

His face becomes serene - well, as serene as his hellish appearance can get - and he gets up with a deceptive quickness for his massive size that is quite impressive to see in action.

"I's gotta git my kill room ready, but I'll sees yuh later, Miss Morticia!"

And with that, he blows me a kiss and heads towards his Redroom, to do something very heinous to some poor, unsuspecting whore. I chuckle to myself and think that today has been great, when out of thin air, Pat Bale strides in with that gait of his, like he's Rick fucking Flair. I half expect him to say, "WOOOO!" Well, the day *was* going great, I thought.

Out of the corner of my eye, I watch him slither over to the pop machine to get himself a Coke Zero. The entire time he leers at me like the predator he truly is. He is so fucking disgusting. I mean, he is a beautiful man that is always looking amazing from head to toe, but he is just a fucking psychopath, and his murders are already legend here. I've heard enough horror tales of what he does to children and women to know that he is evil incarnate.

Just the other day, before his vacation, he took a blowtorch to an eleven-year old's vagina and anus while he used a cheese grater to grind and peel away the poor child's nonexistent breasts. And that was just his foreplay. I can't deal with his maniacal ass, so I pull out my ragged, dog-eared copy of Dead Inside, and begin reading and underlining my favorite passages just so I don't have to converse with his creepy, nutcase ass. A good ten minutes have ticked by, and I'm fully immersed in the story until he begins speaking.

"What are you reading there?"

"A book."

"Oh really? How very droll. I never could have guessed a book."

"Can't get nothing past you," I say, with all the enthusiasm of a man being led to the gallows.

I can feel him directly behind me now; his presence fully permeates the room with a kind of darkness that wasn't there before, like a toxic, poisonous cloud.

"Dead Inside, huh? Care to elaborate on its premise?"

"It is about a security guard who fucks corpses and a pediatric doctor who eats dead babies."

"Sounds like me."

"I said eat, not fuck it."

"To-may-to, to-mah-to, same game."

"Same game? It's not even the same ballpark, psycho-boy, not even the same league," I piff in annoyance. He doesn't need to know the narrator fucks a baby to pieces in the book since I'm trying to not have a real conversation with him.

"Whatever, amateurs fuck dead ones. It's no fun unless you can drink in their fear and pain."

"Whatever you say there, supreme edgelord."

"Wait a minute," Pat interrupts,

"You said the book is called Dead Inside, right?"

"Yeah...so?"

"I just killed the writer last night, I believe."

"Get the fuck out of here."

"No wait, I'm serious," says Pat, showcasing a large, shit-eating grin from ear to ear.

"Yeah, you just so happened to kill my favorite author last night, I am sooo sure."

"Chandler something, right?"

"Morrison," I murmur, almost to myself.

"That's it!"

"Last night, I decided to walk a bit after I made a brief appearance at Kendall Roy's fortieth birthday party; way too extravagant, in my humble opinion, by the way. Anyway, I wanted to walk home, and maybe kill a whore or a hobo, when I was passing by my favorite restaurant Dorsia...try the swordfish meatloaf with onion marmalade, it's exquisite! Wait, what am I saying, you could never set foot in there, well, unless you were my date, of course!"

"Is there a point to this ultra-fascinating story, Pat?"

"All my stories have a point, Morticia. Catch up. As I was saying, I was strolling past when I heard this pathetic fellow squawking how he is the groundbreaking, transgressive genius author of Dead Inside and how dare they not let him in. It would have been hilarious if it wasn't so earth-shattering cringeworthy. The host told him that he was extremely sorry, but getting in tonight, or the foreseeable future, would be problematic at best for him, and to please stop making a scene. It would seem your literary idol is nothing but a pretentious cad."

I try to picture that scenario, and to be honest I'm incredulous. I mean he's a big-time writer after all, Pat is making him sound like a buffoon. I've perused all his Twitter posts, and he comes off as too cool for school. Of course, Pat is making this shit up. I am Jack's skeptical disbelief.

"As I was saying, his look of utter sadness as he dejectedly walked away was breathtaking. I could see he was just a tourist, there are no rock star author's anymore, no money in it. Your brooding novelist could never be in my shoes, they are Alessandro Galet Scritto Leather Oxford's, $2,400 a pair. I have four sets! He couldn't afford one. At that exact moment, I knew I was going to kill him, and I was going to do it for you, Morticia."

"For me? Then you must not know a thing about me, he's my favorite author in the world. I'd never want him dead in a million years, bucko."

"Then, you should know the saying of never meet your heroes. The minute you put someone on a pedestal, they have total power over you. No one is worth putting on a pedestal. He would have only disappointed you anyway. He puts on a false persona, fabricated to sell his *brand* on social media. Nothing more, nothing less."

I stare into Pat's unblinking, dark eyes. It feels like looking into the eyes of a cadaver, it is like gazing into nothingness, just an empty void. Maybe Pat has a point, hell, even a broken clock is right twice a day. I couldn't even convey how much effort I went into promoting Morrison's work when I wasn't busy killing the male scum of the earth. I always tried to do a witty tweet, or include him in my mentions, half the time he barely even acknowledged me, or liked my posts. He probably had me on mute or something. Bret Easton Ellis had mentioned once, that to make great art, you had to be a bastard. I'm paraphrasing, of course, but you get the gist of it.

"Earth to Morticia," Pat barked, violently pulling me out of my thoughts.

"As I was saying, I followed closely behind him until we got close to a long, dark alley. As he strode past its entryway, I shoved him into it with all my might. He fell into a puddle of rainwater with a startled yelp, scaring off a large sized, gray rat munching on a moldy slice of bagel. I sprung behind him, putting a rear naked choke around his scrawny, chicken neck, and hissed into his ear that he would never be anything other than a hack, and would never be like his literary idols. No Hemingway, Bukowski, and no Joan Didion.

"He started blubbering like a little girl with a skinned shin, which didn't surprise me. I straddled him, using my knees on both of his shoulders to subdue him. I produced my favorite knife from my Brunello Cucinelli slacks, a Falcon Stiletto, and menacingly pointed it at him. Just as I was preparing for a bit of the old ultraviolence, a wheezing cough startled me out of my impending bloodlust. I sprang forward, knife in hand, ready to dispatch this hidden interloper. What I find is a grizzled old man using an ancient refrigerator cardboard box as his humble abode. He stared at me with unblinking, cataract eyes as he consumed a cold hotdog with no bun.

"'Don't mind me, sonny,' the archaic wino said to me with a chuckle.

"'What's your name, hobo?' I asked.

"'The name is Daniel, mister. Daniel J. Volpe.'

"'Well, Daniel, how would you like to make one thousand dollars?'

"'I would like that very much, Sir, that could buy me a bunch of my favorite vices and keep me high enough that I forget all about my shit life.'

"'Fantastic to hear, my new filthy friend. All you must do to earn your bounty is come over here to this useless cretin, defecate AND urinate into his sobbing gullet.'

"Just as I said that, Chandler begins to weep all over again, begging for me not to let this happen, and to just let him go. I answered him by punching him directly in the nose, breaking it. He began choking on his own blood, which amused me greatly.

"'So, Daniel, how about you trotting your ancient ass down here, and earn yourself a big pay day, my wretch of a friend?'

"Daniel began walking towards us like a drunken sailor, obviously already under the influence of many vices. I finally saw him up close, and he was just as disgusting as I had hoped for. He reminded me of a skeleton dipped in yellow candle wax. His skin had all the tell-tale signs of an alcoholic and habitual drug abuser. You could literally see fleas leaping off his shaggy form. Daniel was standing above Chandler's head, he looked down, and gave a crooked grin as he began to pull down his pants. Daniel had no underwear on underneath his slacks, so he was standing nude in front of us now. He had a nest of lice living in his more than ample pubic hair. His rather unimpressive dick stayed mostly hidden in the unwashed nest, thankfully. What didn't stay hidden, though, was the fetid stench that emanated from every orifice of his filthy, unwashed body. In fact, he reeked of sweat, shit, and urine so badly that my eyes began to water uncontrollably from this walking, human trash heap.

"Chandler tried to abscond from Daniel as he approached, but a rapid succession of punches to his kidneys nullified his escape rather quickly. Daniel hovered his shit-caked rectum right above the hapless author's broken nose and mouth. The vagrant began to grunt and strain with real gusto! I watched in rapt fascination, as corded veins become visible on his neck and even his forehead.

"After a few more grunts, followed by some noxious gas, Daniel's anus belched forth a steaming torrent of watery turds and frothy diarrhea directly into the writer's horrified face as I cackled with wild abandon. After Daniel finished with his highly successful defecation, he turned around, pointed his miniscule cock towards the author's face and began to spew, what appeared to me, like a gallon's worth of the most putrid smelling urine I've ever had the displeasure of sniffing. It had the color of fermenting apple cider. The sheer force of the urine being sprayed directly into the writer's feces-encrusted mouth caused him to swallow most of it in order to avoid being waterboarded to death. My God, I couldn't have planned this any better!

"'I'll take my pay now, mister,' Daniel grinned with an outstretched hand, the other tapping his penis nonchalantly, getting the last few drops of piss out of his system.

"'Daniel, my homeless friend, it was worth every penny.'

"I watched as the derelict's eyes widened to the size of dinner plates once I handed him a wad of cash that could have choked a horse. I could almost see his thoughts, already fantasizing about the bag of heroin or meth rocks that he was about to go procure from that lanky, sixteen-year-old brotha' down the street with his jeans falling off his ass. I watched as he disappeared from my vision before I gazed back down at this valueless human being that lay before me. His shit-coated mouth was making guttural, pig like noises that reminded me of a death metal vocalist. I pulled out my trusty stiletto and began to stab his face repeatedly, punching numerous holes into the flesh of his shocked and screaming face. I raggedly cut his throat for good measure and watched the steaming blood fountain out into the cold night air. His body convulsed as his jugular frantically pumped his life force onto the dank alley floor. I wiped his blood from my knife, using his cheap suit like a hand towel. Having my bloodlust satiated, I headed home, whistling a Huey Lewis and The News tune."

I just stare at Pat stupidly, unsure what to think now. He loved to play mental warfare with me, and Lurch constantly. He derives so much pleasure from the abuse he heaps on the two of us. He's like the bastard stepdad we never wanted or asked for, after our mother remarried for the umpteenth time. I know he hates that we are needed here, and that we can fill a role that he could never fulfill on his own. He may be the star quarterback at this place, but that only makes Lurch and I the star running backs. Gross, I just made a fucking sport's analogy. Kill me now, SIGH.

"Cute story, dude, but all I have to do is search his name in the news and prove you wrong instantly."

Pat rises from his chair and smirks at me, the hairs on my arm standing up like electricity has jolted through me. He had a way of freaking a person out. I mean I'm a few sandwiches short of a picnic, but this motherfucker is crazier than Charles Manson eating a bowl of Fruit Loops on your front porch!

"No, not really. You see, I took a moment to investigate your hero's wallet and guess what? He used a pseudonym, that's not even his real name. Sad that I know it and you don't, right? He must have been so embarrassed of the pulpy trash he wrote, passing it off as deep, when in fact it was nothing more than second-rate Splatterpunk cringe."

And with that, he strides away in that annoying, cocksure way that he has, like he is fucking invincible. All the while sporting his grotesque shit-eating grin. A tear escapes my eye as I'm seething inside, I've never wanted to hurt someone so bad in my entire life. And not just hurt, I'm talking total fucking annihilation. My next snuff victim is going to feel my unquenchable wrath, thanks to this walking, talking hemorrhoid. His miserable life is on borrowed time now.

Lux would kill me if anything happened to his star child fucker, but I have never let anyone survive fucking with me, except once in high school. I made a vow to never let that happen to me ever again. Thoughts of the past briefly fill my mind, and I picture Kim White momentarily, before I mentally cast her from my mind almost as quickly as she entered it. When the time is right, this bad bitch is going to strike that asshole down harder than a King cobra. Pat Bale is as good as dead, he is just too stupid to know it yet...

# Chapter Seven

# Lurch's Tape

Rachael Binger Mason woke up in excruciating pain. She's totally nude and has two large meat hooks deeply imbedded into each side of her plump, tender ass cheeks. They are stretched to maximum capacity, almost to the point of the meat ripping from the bone due to the tension being administered from the medical grade, stainless steel hooks. She is on her back in an exceptionally uncomfortable and compromising position, so that her ass faces skyward while all her weight is resting heavily on her aching and strained lower back. Tears of blood cries down her jittering, sweat soaked thighs. Her body is fighting a losing battle trying to handle the abuse being hurled at it. The human frame can only take so much, after all. The sound of movement behind her causes her to squeal in fear and strain her neck to see what is making the ruckus. The sight her tired, bloodshot eyes reveals makes her wish she didn't. Standing in front of her is a creature pulled from her worst nightmares. A musclebound being, of immense size and strength, grins at her with teeth that resembled a shark's more than a human.

"Well good morning, Miss Rachael," the thing says heartily.

"I's thought ya was gonna sleep the day away, yes sirree, Bob!"

The beast in front of her speaks, a kind of hillbilly, redneck speech. The worst part is it sounds so friendly even though the creature has to be the one responsible for putting her into this painful predicament. She is about to address the monstrosity standing in front of her when its muscle strewn arm lashes out with the speed of an anaconda's strike, ripping off her right nipple, and areola with the casual ease of removing a wet band aid. It's so fast, in fact, she doesn't initially even feel any pain.

"I loves me some tittymeat, I chew on it like some fine 'backer."

Slobber forms in the corner of its mouth as her still erect nipple protrudes from its chapped lips. Unfortunately, that isn't the only erect thing. Rachael sees a cock that rivals a horse's, it's heavily vein-laden and twitching already, a copious amount of precum dripping obscenely from its uncut dick hole, like a dog with a serious drooling problem. The creature hums a jaunty tune as it grabs a box of Rice Crispies from the table and dumps the entire container into her gaping and bloody asshole. The sugary cereal mixes with her coagulated blood and remnants of her bout of heavy diarrhea from earlier. Still humming, the beast dumps an entire gallon of vitamin D milk right inside of her already stuffed anal cavity. The milk is extremely cold, sending shivers down her spine. The cereal begins its process of snapping, crackling, and yes, popping inside of her anal cavity. It feels strangely pleasant to Racheal, regardless of the terrifying situation she finds herself in. The beast produces a large wooden ladle, and devours the meal with great relish, as Rachael squeals in equal amounts of horror and revulsion. Heaping spoonful's go down the gullet of the creature with amazing voracity.

The abomination annihilates the cereal in what seems like nanoseconds to her, even though she was filled to the brim mere moments earlier. It takes her ass with both of its giant hands and buries its misshapen face into her heavily damaged bunghole. The fiend laps up the bloody, dingle-berry filled, shit-stained concoction like he has been lost in the desert and was just handed an ice-cold glass of refreshing water. The further it sticks its giant, bulbous head and tongue into her quivering cavity, she feels her tendons begin to rip more and more, reluctantly giving way to this thing's inhuman desire to get every single morsel of cereal and milk out of her battered and raw rectum.

Rachael feels her taint start to rip apart, as her damaged ass meat yawns wider, like a cat just awakening from a long nap. It becomes apparent that her vagina is going to turn into one giant, grizzly orifice for this monstrosity to rape and abuse. A real-life axe wound, as opposed to the metaphorical kind.

"I think my pecker might fit in yuh now!"

"Please, I beg you, don't do this!"

"But this is my job, Miss Racheal," the thing says in an almost comical way.

"Just let me get my nut on camera and then I'll kill ya, okay?"

Racheal's mind feels like it is going to teeter into madness as she watches this hillbilly creature's dick go from a semi-terrifying size, to utterly unreal, right before her terror-stricken eyes. The beast spits a mouthful of brown phlegm into its palm and starts stroking its cock to its magnificent, fully erect potential. It looks like it can get an elephant off without any problem. His colossal cock is going to split her apart in no time, that much is obvious to her.

"I can see you look scared, but I won't just jam it in, no, ma'am, I's gonna lube it up nice and good fer ya!"

And with that it coughs and spits up a copious amount of the brown phlegm, from deep within its lungs, directly onto her cunt and asshole in equal amounts, covering them both up with the gelatinous, gross gunk. And with the lubrication out of the way, her rapist pops its cock deep within her heavily wounded asshole. He needn't have fussed about the lube; her asshole rips wide open from the creature's gargantuan penis. Blood so dark, it is almost black pumps out in earnest, giving the creature easy access deep within her, perforating her bowels in the process. It jackhammers her newly-formed orifice into oblivion. She can feel numerous organs being turned to mincemeat from the creature's unforgiving cock. Blood flows heavily from her mouth and cunt as she fades from literally being fucked to death.

Right before she dies, she feels the creature tense up, and let out a guttural cry as it fills her up with its ungodly semen. She can hear her innards slosh around from the immense amount of inbred baby batter that is filling her body. Incredibly, its vile splooge even starts gushing out of her mouth. When the beast removes its third arm from her ruined sex, pieces of intestine and organs follow with it. The last thing Racheal sees before she dies is the creature going to its worktable and fetching a mallet. Still whistling a cheerful tune, it ambles back to Racheal, and bashes on her head repeatedly, until it is nearly split in two.

# Chapter Eight

# Kim Gets Warmer

The sight of a man having true fear in their eyes from a woman never grows tiresome for me. And that's just the look I'm receiving from Seth the moment I walk into his office. Seth runs the city in terms of its illegal needs, be it drugs, prostitution, murder, anything nefarious whatsoever. You name the price; Seth provides the vice. His look of utter dismay is all I needed to see to confirm he knows exactly what happened to my brother.

"Kim, what a pleasant sur...."

That's all he gets out before I grip his throat with every fiber of my strength and put a blade underneath it.

"Kim...you...don't...have...to...do...this..."

"I need to find Morticia Maggot, that Goth whore was the last one seen with my brother, and now he is missing. He won't return my calls or texts. I know that nothing happens around here without you at least hearing about it."

"Kim, please quit choking me, I'll talk."

I relinquish my death grip on his birdlike, scrawny neck, allowing this prick a momentary reprieve.

"Start talking," I command.

After a moment of Seth massaging his throat, and grimacing in pain, he looks at me dejectedly.

"Look, I'm sorry to be the one to tell you this, but even if you want to take Morticia out, that is an impossibility now. She's rolling with Lux and has his protection. She is untouchable."

"You mean she works for Hurt 2 The Core, that snuff and child porn place?"

"That's the place, they blew the fuck up after that Daisy's Destruction video went viral on the Deep Web. They have every degenerate with a sick fetish paying them top dollar for their filth. Lux is the man now, in terms of power."

I look at him doubtfully before I speak again.

"Tanner's dead because of this, and I want payback, and I'm going to take it out of that Hot Topic hood rat Morticia."

"I'm telling you, Kim, you can't even get to her, word on the street is that she's on lockdown at the H2TC compound. She never leaves."

"Then, I guess you're going to have to get me in there, Seth."

I visibly see the thug in front of me pale from my request. His Adam's apple begins to bob up and down uncontrollably, and his brow begins to sweat.

"Look, Kim," Seth says,

"I don't want to be hacked apart by his machete wielding psychopaths, or have my genitals fed to pit bulls. These fuckers will go medieval on my ass!"

"Then, get me inside the compound. I know they need a surplus of female victims if their producing a lot of this snuff shit."

"Yeah, I could make that happen," Seth stammers.

"But you won't go to Morticia, she only kills the male victims. You'd go to either this mutated, backwoods fuck named Lurch, or this ultra-crazy fucker named Pat Bale. Both are super dangerous!"

"You know I can handle myself, Seth, I'm a big girl. I'll kill whoever is in my way of snuffing this cunt out. I have a trick up my sleeve, remember, I can't feel any pain. All I must do is lull them into thinking they have your typical damsel in distress. After that, either one of these pricks are worm food."

"I know you can handle anyone, Kim, let me reach out to my contact. I'll have some info on where the drop spot location is soon."

"Don't keep me waiting too long though, Seth. I'm in a vendetta type of mood and anyone could die painfully at any second, if you get my meaning."

The look on his face was more than enough to know he got my drift. I headed out into the night with a smile on my face. I was putting myself into a very deadly situation. I have a good chance of not surviving this. Funny that it makes me feel more alive than I have felt in years.

# Chapter Nine

---

# Calm Before The Storm

It's movie night, so Lurch sits in my room, his immense bulk somehow not collapsing my chair. He's looking at me in a peculiar way.

"Something wrong, buddy?"

"I'm worried about ya is all, Miss Morticia."

"Lurch, baby, in case you haven't noticed, I'm one tough cookie, plus I have you, my guardian angel!" As I say that, his face blossoms with the widest grin, he blushes and almost looks demure in my eyes.

"Pat wants to hurt you, I'm jus' so scared for ya."

"I think the two of us can handle his psychotic ass, buddy."

Lurch looks directly into my eyes, tears already dropping from his. He looks apologetic and embarrassed at the same time.

"Miss Morticia, I'm so scared of him. He is the scariest man I ever met, next to my Paw that is. Probably cuz they both love to hurt little ones so much."

I see a flicker of some past atrocity that Lurch's father probably unleashed on him, pass in his eyes before he wipes the tears away from his face. He brushes at his forehead like he is trying to erase a painful memory. I give the big guy a bear hug and tell him everything is going to be okay.

"I'm gonna be a brave boy for you."

"I know you will."

"I won't let him hurt you anymore."

"Well, the same goes for you too, big boy."

"This world is a tough place if you're alone. I guess destiny put us in one another's life for a reason."

Lurch grins down at me and pats my head gently with his giant hand.

"Friends forever, Miss Morticia!"

"Yes, Lurch, friends forever! Now, let's stop all this mushy stuff and get movie night going! What's your pick this week buddy?"

Lurch scratches his chin and goes over to the DVD shelf to make his pick. I'm curious as to what he will opt for. I don't have to wait long before he hands me his selection. I can't help but titter inwardly at the movie he brings back to me.

"The Last Unicorn again?"

"Yessum."

I shrug and pop the disc into the player. I grab our tubs of popcorn and sit at the end of my bed. I beckon Lurch to come sit next to me by patting on the mattress beside me, and he happily obliges. As the film begins, the giant sits transfixed by the outstanding animation and story. A part of me wants to chill, and enjoy the flick, but another part of me can't shake the thought that I am on borrowed time somehow.

***

I totally understand why Lurch is nervous around Pat. Lately, he has been coming onto me way harder than usual. I'm not sure what has caused it since I act like he doesn't exist for the most part. He makes me throw up in my mouth every time he tries to flirt with me. That's probably the reason though. Like the Nine Inch Nails song, he just wants something he can never have. But his flirting is more terrifying than flattering since he is a fucking sociopath. I think he wants to rape, torture, and kill me and knowing him, it's not in that order. Lurch feels it too, hence why he's stuck to my back like a coat.

I think I'm going to have to kill him, which will probably make Lux have someone kill me too. I know his life is worth more than mine, at least in the eyes of Hurt 2 The Core Productions. That's why me and Lurch need to get the fuck out of dodge. I'm not quite sure where our futures ultimately lie, but it's no longer here, that I'm sure of. Luckily, I've barely spent a dime of my money here, except on some movies and books; necessities, you know? I'm not even sure Lurch gets paid but that's ok. I've got plenty of money for us both to start over. I pause the movie and take Lurch's hand. He looks at me questioningly.

"What do you say about us getting out of here for real and starting over somewhere else?"

"Really? You'd take me too, Miss Morticia?"

"Of course, Lurch, you're my bestie!"

"Well, okay!"

He gives me a sloppy kiss on my forehead, and I start the movie. Everything seems perfect in the world right now.

I am Jack's foolish optimism.

# Chapter Ten

# A Fly On The Wall

I listen intently to the conversation going on between Morticia and that retard behind her closed door. So, this stupid cunt thinks she's going to get the upper hand on me and kill me with the help of her oversized infantile hooligan? Well guess what? I am going to be on my *"A"* game from here on out. Plus, I am going to strike so hard and fast, they won't even know what happened. The Bighead, I'll take out quick. Being speedy and merciless is the only way to make sure that muscle bound, shit-kicking simpleton can't overpower me. Then, I can have all the time in the world to torture Morticia. I can't wait to taste that uppity Goth whore's blood, and to see what her insides look like, as I slowly dismantle her body, piece by piece.

Lux will chew me out, of course, but I've been chewed out before. These nobodies can be replaced. I'm the goddamned star here. Nobody can replicate what I do here. No one has the stomach or limitless levels of depravity. The other day, I pulled out a premature baby, fucked it until it was in pieces, then put it in a blender. I pureed it into liquid paste and made the shell-shocked mother drink every bit of it down to the last drop. And that was only the beginning.

Once the inane video they were watching started back up, I headed for the elevator to go pick up some supplies for my video shoot for tomorrow and get my plan in action. These two were on borrowed time now. My cock stiffens as I imagine all the carnage that I have planned for Morticia. I will teach her a lesson about being a snooty bitch to me. Nobody snubs Pat Bale, and if they do, they never get to make that mistake to me, or anyone else ever again.

Game on, fuckers.

# Chapter Eleven

# Pat's Tape

Lindsay Crook comes to with a start. She awoke from a terrifying dream where a blank faced man has abducted her while she was out walking her Morkie puppy, Oliver, before bedtime. The faceless cretin stomped her dog to death before drugging her with a rag doused in chloroform. The sounds of the dog's agony followed her as she sank down into pitch-black oblivion. Now that she's alert, despair crushes her in its vice like grip. It's all real. She can't move. She's shackled to an archaic looking gynecologists' examination table with barbed wire wrapped tightly around her wrists and her ankles.

It cuts deeply into her tender flesh every time she moves, no matter how miniscule her efforts are. She can see the glistening exposed meat underneath her skin, a small but steady flow of blood pools around her injured limbs. She is nude, her legs spread wide, a lewd pose that shows off every inch of her young, supple form, to the unblinking video camera that is set up in front of her. It is incredibly hot in the room. Her sweaty hair is matted on her face like she just dived into a pool. Her skin gleams like she had just rubbed baby oil all over herself. It looks and feels like Hell in here.

There are blood-caked tables and an array of deadly-looking weapons strewn about haphazardly. Lindsay sees movement out of the corner of her vision and whips her head quickly towards it. A very handsome, and very nude, man stands in the corner. He has a menacing look on his face, the smile is more predatory than friendly, wolfish almost. Lindsay sadly notices that the strangers' cock is totally engorged with blood and excitement. It's obvious to her that this person is going to hurt her. Fleeting hopes of getting out of this predicament dissipates like the shadows when a light is cast onto it.

The man comes closer to her; he looks like a magazine model. Impeccable hair gelled into place on a face that could turn any woman's head. A muscular, athletic body, graced with abs for days. He has an above average penis that looks like it was cast in granite. On any other day, this would be a hot, sexual fantasy, but in this macabre dungeon, it is more like a nightmare. His most terrifying trait has to be his eyes, she supposes. It reminds her of a documentary on Great White sharks. They have a black, soulless look to them. They are not the eyes of a human being. They are the eyes of an apex predator, and Lindsay is his prey.

"Well, hello there, Lindsay! I'm glad you are awake now, a few moments longer and I figured I might need to start carving you up with my trusty fillet knife here to rouse you from dreamland"

"Please," Lindsay frightfully begins, before being violently struck in the mouth by a closed-handed fist.

"There will be no humanity found in here, cunt. No quick, merciful death either. I hate women. Snuffing them out painfully, one by one, is my one true joy. And no amount of talking, crying, or begging is going to get you out of my grasp, the sooner you understand that, and accept your fate, the better."

Lindsay lashes out violently against her restraints, causing the razor wire to bite even further into her tender flesh. The pain is blinding in its total ferocity. But no matter how hard she fights against her restraints; it is a losing battle. Slowly, it dawns on Lindsay that the man is talking to her again.

"Earth to Lindsay," the man says with a lupine grin from ear to ear.

"Huh?" Lindsay says, almost to herself, still shaking off the mental fog caused by her captor's fierce strike to her cranium.

Lindsay understands the words coming out of the man's lips but can't fathom how a human being could utter such cruelties with such casual abandon. As Lindsay gets lost again in her own thoughts, a thunderous slap rocks her back into the present nightmare she finds herself in.

"I'm sorry, did I break your concentration, bitch?" That disgusting smile covers his face like a heinous mask once again. He spits a huge phlegm wad directly into Lindsay's face. The loogie splatters into her left eye with an audible *THWACK*. It is the same consistency of drool from a Great Bernard dog. Brownish in color with flecks of red throughout, presumably blood.

"I want you to feel agony like you've never experienced before. I will try my best to prolong your miserable life to the best of my abilities, that is a promise, Lindsay."

The lunatic saunters over to the worktable, and surveys the weaponry lovingly, as if looking at his true love before he selects a satchel and brings it back towards Lindsay.

"Are you at all familiar with serial killers, you worthless whore? I know most women love to listen to and watch true crime podcasts; it's probably because deep down, all women want to be victimized by men."

Lindsay just stares at the man wordlessly, unsure on the next right move to take. In the blink of an eye, he begins to throttle her throat viciously. Her capillaries burst in her eyes as her airway desperately tries to eek what little air it can. When Lindsay's face is about the same hue as a ripe eggplant, and death felt like it was inside the room with her, almost touching her, he relinquishes his grip on her raw throat. Sweet, beautiful air once again fills her lungs. She coughs uncontrollably from the pain savaging her poor throat.

"Sorry, I just hate women so much. I didn't mean to choke you that long. I almost lost control and killed you way too quickly. I have a few things I'd love to do to you before you die a horrible death. Hopefully, I can make you last long enough, if I just manage to maintain my composure."

He chuckles to himself as he walks to a boom box sitting on the worktable and turns it on. In The Air Tonight, by Phil Collins, starts to play, making the whole scenario even more ludicrous to the tormented and frightened girl.

"Now, as I was saying before I rudely interrupted myself. Are you familiar with serial killers? No? I most definitely am. I'm what you might call a connoisseur. One of my favorites is Albert Fish. The pure joy he derived from the murder, defilement, and eventual dismemberment and consumption of ten-year-old Grace Budd is still a subject that brings me a lot of joy, especially the note he sent Grace's mother afterwards, killing her still with his words, almost like he was able to murder her twice!"

He unrolls the satchel, and tenderly, stares at the tools inside of it. Gleaming knives, scalpels, and other items used for butchery fills her with utter despair.

"Now, Albert Fish called his tools of the trade, Implements *of Hell,* an apt title if I ever heard one, don't you agree, worthless sow?"

Lindsay knows better than to ignore this human-shaped fiend and quickly nods her head in affirmation. The horrible smile is painted across his face again, her blood feels like ice is running through her veins. Through this maniac's hands is her inevitable and ugly death. It will not be a quick or merciful one.

"Have you ever heard of FGM, pig?" Lindsay just stares at the man as if he is some rare and frightening arachnid. Lindsay slowly shakes her head *'no'* in reply.

"It stands for female genital mutilation, and ninety seven percent of girls, ages fifteen to forty-nine, have this happen to them in Guinea, West Africa alone. A circumciser uses a blade and cuts off a girls' clitoris. Sometimes, a circumciser will carve up to thirty pussies in a row using the same blade. Now, that sounds like a dream job, am I right? It is mainly done to control a woman's sexuality. I wholeheartedly agree with this process. Women are nothing but cum receptacles, strictly for the gratification of a man's pleasure, nothing more. I was initially going to sodomize you with a bat covered in broken glass, but I've changed my mind. That bit of foreplay is going to be bestowed on a special, little, gothic cunt I have had my eye on for a while now. As for you, you dirty trollop, I only have boundless amounts of pain and torment in store for you. Now, let's get that pesky clitoris out of the equation first, shall we?"

Lindsay stares in abject horror as he pilfers through his arsenal, his digits affectionately probing each of his blades like a lover would. He finally seems to decide on a cutting tool and brings it up to Lindsay's face for her to see. It is an old Swiss Army knife, its once vibrant red handle now sullied from old age. The blade looks extremely dull, and it is covered in an abundance of rust.

Like the striking power of a champion pugilist, the man's hands shoot out with a blurring speed. He is halfway done gleefully cutting off her clitoral hood in the blink of an eye. A guttural garble of pleas and screeches vomit forth from Lindsay's pain-racked face. The knife being used to cut through her lady parts is highly insufficient for the job, probably the exact reason it was selected, to be sure. Blood runs down into her vaginal canal and her anus as the man laboriously saws at her anatomy like one would a tree branch.

The same body part that brought her countless bouts of pleasure in this world, is now responsible for this maddening pain threatening to make her pass out yet again. She longs for the darkness to overtake her. With a flurry of hacks, her clitoris is successfully removed from her body. She watches dumbstruck as the madman forces it down her throat, and then clamps a blood-coated hand over her mouth, until she is forced to swallow it or suffocate.

"Don't say I never gave you anything," he chides.

Lindsay looks at her captor in defeat and simply says, "Kill me, please."

He looks at her for a moment or two, before going to the worktable, and coming back with a pair of once white cotton panties that are now more rust colored. He proceeds to stuff them into her trembling mouth until she gags uncontrollably.

"I only want to hear your pain; your words do nothing but fall on deaf ears, bitch."

Once again, he leaves Lindsay in search of something. When he comes back with his new object in tow, she isn't immediately sure what he is going to do with it. A moment later, it dawns on her, and she bucks, and furiously shake her head in terror. It is an above average-size wine bottle, and she knows where it is going to end up. A heart wrenching, muffled scream pierces the room. The man only smiles back, relishing her terror.

"Let's finish dismantling this axe wound of yours forever, shall we?"

The mouth of the wine bottle is cold as it is positioned against her pussy. She feels it slide into her folds as it pen-etrates her. It is a tight fit already due to its enormous size. She doubts he can fit it into her, until he takes the sole of his shoe, and uses all his leg strength to push it deeper inside of her vagina. As the bottle delves deeper into Lindsay, it makes sounds that remind her of wearing her rain boots and playing in the thick mud as a young girl. The body of the bottle is deep inside of her now. Her pubic region takes on a swollen, pregnant look, like a grisly, reverse childbirth. With one final grunt of exertion, the heel, and base of the bottle are swallowed fully into her gaping cunt hole. The pain is cataclysmic.

The discomfort causes her brain to momentarily shut down, giving her a brief reprieve from all this agony. That is, until he begins to pummel her lower body with a two-by-four. The furious reign of blows directed at her pubic region shatters the bottle inside her as he beats her with the unyielding piece of wood. Broken glass slice through her vaginal lips and lower abdomen as it makes its reappearance like a magician's rabbit at a kid's birthday party. He continues to strike her, even as her vagina burps up ghastly blood clots entangled in the punishing glass. A piece of her bowel peeks out from a particularly deep gash in her belly. Lindsay feels the world is dimming around her.

The pain is all encompassing now. She knows the man is talking to her, but she is only able to focus on the searing pain, until he looks her dead in her eyes, face to face with her, and sinks his teeth into her nose. He savagely rips, and tears, shaking his head mercilessly like a Pit-bull does as it latches onto weaker prey. With a mighty heave, her nose tears away from her face, adding another flood of pain into her already demolished body. He looks down on her as he munches on her appendage like an apple before he lets it fall to the ground.

"I know you are fading fast," he says, "But there is one more thing I would like to do to you before you die. How does immolation sound to you?"

He procures a gas can from somewhere out of Lindsay's line of vision and pours the noxious liquid all over her nude and mangled form. He produces a box of matches and does that thing they do in the movies that always fascinated her growing up. He snaps his fingers and the match burns to life, as if by sorcery.

A moment later, he tosses it at her, bathing her in the scorching pain of the fire immediately. As her physique begin to blister and darken, the flames lick and nibble at her delicate body as if they are in the throes of lovemaking. Lindsay's frame bucks ferociously against her restraints as her form begins to cook. The flames quickly race up to her terrified face before engulfing her entire head, burning her hair, and cooking her eyeballs, before they violently pop from her skull. Her facial features begin to melt and slide down her neck like she is a human candle. As she mercifully begins to die, she realizes two things simultaneously.

Number one was that God never did come and save her like she wished and prayed. She was a devout Catholic all her life and still God has forsaken her. He let her feel everything, much like Jesus had. Either, he truly is a vengeful God, or he simply does not exist. She is about to find out the answer to that eternal question herself, and it terrifies her to her very core. The second thing she knows, as she begins to pass away, is that her killer is pissing all over her face. She doesn't need her eyes to know what he is doing. Now that her vision is gone, and her nose has been savagely excised, her sense of hearing is more pronounced than ever in her fleeting, final moments. His maniacal laughter follows her as the darkness swallows Lindsay, once and for all, freeing her from her killer's deadly grasp for eternity.

# Chapter Twelve

---

# A Hopeful Future

I can see Lurch in the kitchen, at his usual spot near the lone window, in the underground area. Its thick, black bars look more at home in a prison than in a lunchroom, but I guess that is basically what we are in though, isn't it? I can see the vast man drawing something with his crayons. Upon closer scrutiny, I see it is him and I holding hands in what looks like a forest by a cabin. It's what we talked about earlier, our big dream once we leave this place. As I sit next to him, I can see he is smiling from ear to ear, no doubt thinking of a bright, hopeful future.

"Hey buddy, how are you doing?"

"I'm great, Miss Morticia, jus' thinkin' bout our new life, so I's thought I would make a picture, see?"

Lurch happily gives me the drawing, beaming brighter than a kid in their elementary school picture.

"Damn, this is some top-notch artwork here, Lurch. I'm going to put this up in my room!"

"I's made two, gots the other one up myself," the behemoth chuckles.

"Well, I guess that makes us twins then."

He smiles wanly at me and goes back to looking distantly out of the iron clad window again.

"Okay, big boy, what's wrong?"

"Nuthin'."

"You can't lie for shit, Lurch, spill those beans."

The big man looks down at me and sighs heavily.

"When we gonna go, Miss Morticia? This ain't no life fer me no more."

"As soon as I can figure out an idea to get us out of here, bubba. We must be patient and come up with a good plan."

Lurch nods, and huffs silently, continuing to gaze out of the window. I can tell he needs more from me, but unfortunately, that's all I have to give him for now. The truth is, I have no idea how to get us out of here in one piece. I have a feeling Lux will keep us here till I am a shriveled up, crusty, dusty grandmother, with cobwebs covering my poon! Besides, a part of me is very afraid to be in the real world again.

If I am here, I can kill without repercussions. No one can touch me in here. I'm like a goddess inside these walls, my viewership has only grown stronger since I came here. I've received countless fan letters from girls that thank me constantly for dispatching these worthless men. In a world where they feel powerless, I make them feel powerful. I make them feel heard. I validate them.

How can I abandon them when they need me to be their hands of justice? All these thoughts dissipate after I take a deep breath and mentally cast them out. I look lovingly at Lurch, the big goon is still looking outside, like by willing himself outside, it will somehow come to fruition. I give him a hug which snaps him out of his melancholic daydreams. He looks at me and gives me a big ole goofy smile.

"I must go do my stream now, okay, big guy? I will come find you once I dispatch this prick and take a shower afterwards. You can even pick the flick tonight!"

"How's bout Forrest Gump?"

I inwardly cringe at this. I think we've watched this Tom Hanks classic eight times already. It makes him cry by the bucket load, but it also oddly fills him with hope, so I choose not to complain about it. I guess he sees a lot of himself in that simple-minded character.

"It's a date." I blow him a kiss and cause Lurch to turn redder than a can of Coke. He pretends to catch my invisible kiss, and waves back shyly. He then goes back to looking out of the window. I slowly make the trek back towards my Redroom. I have come up with an interesting way to torture my victim in a way fitting of his past indiscretions, and I can't wait to see how it plays out for my lovely viewers!

# Chapter Thirteen

---

# Memory Lane

I's turn my head towards Miss Morticia as she goes in her room to kill sum dirty, womern hating varmint. She's great at killin', better than me fer sure! She comes up with the craziest ideas! I loves Miss Morticia, she and me have been like peanut butter and jelly since she showed up in my life. Before her, when new people arrived, I mostly scared the bejesus outta them cuz of my looks and all. That or they wuz mean to me. It hurt me bad to be all alone here. Mr. Bale has always been a no-good, low-down dog to me. I hates him!!! He makes me feel afraid and I hates that feeling. He makes me feel small like my mean daddy did. At least my grandpappy was around back then to protect me.

   He was like Miss Morticia is now. Lovin' and carin' bouts me. I remember when I was jus' a lil' squirt and I was walkin' home from school. Muh teacher had sent me home and told me not to comes back cuz she said I was too ugly to teach, and that I stunk like hogs rooting' in their manure. I begged her not to do this cuz my daddy told me I ain't nuthin' but an ugly retart, and I really wanted to learn stuff, so he'd be proud of me fer once. Maybe he would even stop beatin' on me so much. I jus' wanted him to love me is all. But no matter what, he seemed like he had no love in his heart fer me.

My teacher grabbed me by my ear, and drug me right outta the class, the sounds of the kids whoopin', and a hollerin' in joy cuz the teacher was being mean, followed me as she threw me out. I started cryin' as I made the long walk home through the woods to my daddy's cabin. I tried to come up with a reason to be home so early, but likes my daddy says, I'm too stupid to knows anything. At least grandpappy would be there to console me, I thought. Grandpappy had come to live with us ever since he blew his legs to smithereens for fishin' with dynamite. He had been in his moonshine, and thought he threw that stick of dynamite into the lake, instead, he dropped it into the boat and *KA-BOOM*! The rest is history. Grandpappy loved me even though I'm so ugly and dumb. He said I always have a good heart and that's more important than bein' a good-lookin' feller. So, I gets to the cabin, and grandpappy is on the deck in his wheelchair, chewin' some chaw. He waves at me as I come closer.

"Howdy, boy, what you doin' home this early in the day?"

"I's got kicked out, Grandpappy."

"Fer What?"

"Bein' ugly I suppose."

"That ain't no reason to be kicked outta learnin', if that was the case there'd be loads of fellers and gals not in school."

"She said I was a distraction to the class."

"Hmmph," huffed Grandpappy, as he spat what seemed like a gallon of his chaw juice all over the faded wood planks on the deck.

I looked around fretfully and asked, "Is my paw around?"

"Nah, he is tryin' to get his dick wet in that worthless cracker gal down the road. He better look out, that sperm burpin', gutter slut ain't nothin' but a trashy whore that's been with every feller in Cowgill, TWICE!"

"Good, I don't want him whoopin' on me jus' yet. My days already so bad, don't need him hurtin' me on top of everything else."

"Boy, yer big enough to whoop ten fellas, when you gonna stand up to yer paw?"

The idea of openin' a can of whoop ass on my paw never even dawned on me!

"Shucks, Grandpappy, a fella ain't supposed to hurt his paw!"

"Well, when a fellers paw ain't worth a pot ta piss in, then maybe they should. Yer a good boy, you got a good heart, but you gotta stand up fer yerself someday, boy!"

"Yessir, Grandpappy."

"Now, why don't you give yer old grandpappy a piggyback ride down to the creek so we can rustle up some viddles fer dinner? Grab our poles, boy, tonight we's havin' us a fish fry!"

I ran to the shed, and grabbed our fishin' poles and my tackle box, then I rushed over to grandpappy, and threw him onto my shoulders like he was bout' the size of a lil' kitten, and off we went, and fer a little while, at least, we had a real swell time, and I forgot about my paw and how mad he would be at me for a spell.

We were headin' back, once it was dusk; we had caught some dandy fish fer dinner, and we was jaw flappin' back and forth about this and that, when all of a sudden, a rock blasted me in my dang forehead. Next thing I knew, I had dropped to the ground, and my poor grandpappy fell hard on his side, on account that I's was still carryin' him. He let out a howl of pain like a beaten dog might. I was fuzzy, and woozy, and on top of that, blood flowed into my eyes which burned em' somethin' fierce. I heard grandpappy warn me about somethin', but I didn't know what. I looked up, and there was my paw, grinnin' like the devil himself. He punched me hard in my little eye and kicked me even harder in my belly.

"Well, if it isn't my worthless, ugly faggot of a son, wanna tell me why you got yer ugly ass kicked out of school?"

I was fittin' to try to explain to him, but before I could even utter a word, he slapped me so hard that it brought tears to my eyes.

"Don't you hurt my grandson, you low down dirty dog," my grandpappy exclaimed fiercely.

"Shut your pie hole old timer, or else I'll tune yer old ass up right with him!"

For a brief second, I felt all the anger well up insides me like flood water, and before I could stop the words from comin' out, they escaped my lips.

"You hurt my grandpappy and I'll tune you up, paw, see if I don't!"

I could tell from my Paw's stern but shocked face, he wasn't expectin' me to stand up to him like I did. Behind me, I heard my grandpappy excitedly voice his approval with a big and boisterous yell.

"Yee-Haw, that's my boy!"

I smiled inwardly, proud of myself in that moment, before I looked at my paw starin' at me like he was lookin' at a deer he was fixin' ta shoot. His face was the color of a tomato from the garden. I knew I was gonna get the whoopin' of my life today. My paw got to me in three quick strides and went to wailing on me for all he was worth. My paw was thin, but he was wiry. He had lived off the land all his life and hard work was all he knew. He was easily the toughest man in all of Caldwell County. I put up my hands, but only to try and muffle the punches he was throwin' at me. I blocked them best I could, but he was raining blows on my face like pelting rain in a thunderstorm. He was killin' me, I thought, all I could see was stars, like in a cartoon.

Just when I thought I was gonna be knocked out cold, I heard my grandpappy scream, "Get yer filthy mitts offa my boy!" and with that, he hit my daddy full force in his noggin with a big stick. It momentarily dazed my paw, givin' me a moment to collect my bearings. Well, that did it, I thought, me and grandpappy were in a quagmire now! My paw seemed shell-shocked that his daddy had walloped him with that stick. He brushed at his forehead where he was struck, and blood was flowing freely from the newly formed gash. He looked at his own blood on his hand and it seemed to incite somethin' in him.

He looked at us demonically and spewed "You old son-of-a-bitch, I'm gonna shove that stick up your scrawny, ancient ass, and then turn it fuckin' sideways!"

At that exact moment, I felt a switch goin' off in my brain. I was tired of bein' scared of my paw. He was a bad man and he had hurt me almost my entire life. I could take that forever, but now, he was gonna hurt my grandpappy. I loved him more than anything in this entire world. Nobody would lay a hand on him if I could help it. He was standing over my grandpappy, he had snatched away the stick and was menacin' him with it. I rose up behind him without a sound; only my grandpappy saw me. Even though he was afraid, he looked me right in the eye, and silently nodded at me, almost sayin' do it, just with his eyes though. I was directly behind him when my foot snapped a twig. My daddy froze in his spot for a second, before he spun around and faced me. He tried to puff out his chest, and look tough, but there was fear in his eyes for the first time when he gazed at me.

"Now, look here, boy, let's just forget about this and go make them dandy lookin' fish you two caught earlier and have us a nice dinner. Shit, I'll even let you have a barley pop!"

Yup, if my paw was offerin' me a beer, he was afraid; the shoe was finally on the other foot!

I continued staring at him for a few more seconds before I grabbed him and lifted him up to my face like he was no heavier than a lil' baby. We were face to face, mine was enraged, but his was petrified. He looked like he was gonna say somethin' tough before I roared at him and sank my teeth deep into his upturned, shocked face. Cords of veins began to pulse in my neck, as I began to snarl, and shake my head back and forth like a rabid dog eatin' a coon. I could hear his flesh beginning to tear loose from his screaming face, like the sound you get when you rip paper into long strips. Blood flowed heavily down his face. It filled my mouth with a coppery taste that only made me work harder at what I was doin'. With one final tug, I felt his face pull free from its fleshy restraints.

The sound reminded me of the time I had to jam my arm up a cow's pussy in order to scoop out the dead baby calf, and broken placenta, inside of it. My paw looked like somethin' out of a dadgum horror film as his skinless face squealed in agony. His meaty, pulpy, beet red appearance glistened in the dusk, like a newly washed and waxed hot rod. His blood continued to plummet from his face, as his eyes began to roll up into his head. Before he died from my attack, I wanted to crush his skull. I placed my giant meat hooks against his head and began to push them together with all my might.

My paw began to gurgle, and fidget in my hands, like someone having a dang seizure. I pushed harder on his skull. One of his eyes began to bulge in its socket, before it burst forth in a spray of multicolored goo, splattering his cheeks in gore. A moment later, his head caved into itself, looking more like a flat basketball than a human head. Brains and skull fragments began to leak freely out of his nose, mouth, and even the newly emptied eye socket. The viscera coated my mitts, like when me and grandpappy had made meatloaf for supper a few weeks back. Once my daddy's body stopped convulsing, I tossed him to the ground like the piece of trash he truly was. Grinning, I spat a big loogie on his unrecognizable face. You couldn't even tell you was lookin' at a human head no more.

"Good job, boy, now, help yer old grandpappy up off this hard ground, my ass is killin' me somethin' fierce!"

"You ain't mad at me, grandpappy?"

"I could never be mad at you sonny, I loves ya. It was him or us. Your daddy had the devil in him ever since he was but a youngin'. He was born plumb bad is all. The world is better off without him, sonny."

I silently nodded in agreement. I went over, lifted grandpappy off the ground, and carried him back to the cabin. Once I had him safely in in his chair, he gave me a hug then spoke, "Now, go bury that worthless wretch of a man out yonder, boy. I'll get the fish ready, and when you get back, we will have a nice dinner together and I'll read you a story before bedtime, ok?"

I told him it sounded dandy and gave him a slobbery kiss on his ancient forehead, before I went outside to the shed and retrieved a shovel. I threw my old man over my shoulder, like a sack of taters, and headed off into the woods to bury him. As I shoveled the dirt away for his makeshift grave, it surprised me how little I felt for him at the end. He may have been my paw in name, but he was more like an enemy or a stranger. I had my grandpappy and that was all I needed.

After the hole was dug, I kicked his worthless corpse into the hollow, and commenced to fillin' the hole back in with the dark, rich soil. As a final insult, I pissed on that devil's grave, just to spite him. Once the job was done, I headed back to the cabin, and enjoyed a yummy fish fry with grandpappy. It's funny how a memory can sneak up on a feller and take him back in time for a spell.

\*\*\*

Grandpappy had lived two more years, before he passed away in his sleep, and left me alone and afraid. I buried him next to my paw's grave. I lived by myself for God knows how long, before a group of Lux's people eventually found me, and the cabin, while they were lookin' for a place to film their nasty flicks in private. At first, they's was gunna jus' kill me with a bullet to my noggin,' and take the cabin fer their murder flicks.

But then, one of the fellers saw my pecker, and got a bright idea. They set up some fancy video camera and brought in this real good lookin' cracker gal.

She was nude as the day she was born. I could see her cooter, and her fun bags, as plain as day, and I started to get myself a real dandy stiffy. They tolds me to fuck her so's I did what the fellers said. Everything was goin' jus' fine, until my ramrod busted up her insides somethin' fierce, and she started spewing out blood out by the dad'gum bucket full! Welp, I didn't want that fine lookin' cracker gal to suffer any more so's I clobbered her head in with a mallet that was layin' on the cabin floor. I sent her brains flying out, littering the dust-covered ground, then, I scooped 'em up and ate them like they were a tasty treat like in a real fancy restaurant!

Those fellers said I was a natural, and said if I did these flicks, they wouldn't kill me. Eventually, they moved their productions to where it is now. Lately, I've been wonderin' if the cabin is still there in Cowgill, Missouri. If it is, then maybe me and Miss Morticia can go live there in peace and quiet. I want to get away from this damn place so bad! I think she will love it there. I can show her where my grandpappy is buried, and we can go fishin' on the lake, and tell stories, and laugh! Smiling about our future, I go back to drawin' and occasionally lookin' out that barred window, imaginin' our future, together forever.

# Chapter Fourteen

# Ass to Mouth

I'm staring up at my latest victim as he begins to snap out of the effects of the sedative, I gave him. I needed to make sure he would stay docile as I set up this rad, albeit Jigsaw-esque trap for this boy-shaped human turd. I mean, my audience demands it! While the others here kill with the best of them, to be sure, I like to add some panache to my shit! Go big or go fucking home! Next to me, on my worktable, I have a massive Super Soaker fully loaded with Lurch's potent piss. Trust me when I say that it is ultra-repugnant to the senses, after all, I loaded the damn thing. I aim it at my somewhat semi-conscious victim and let a barrage of piss bullets shoot into his gaping, drooling mouth, causing him to violently choke and retch. Remnants of his last meal vomit forth in a real gruel gusher, as he frantically fights to regain his gasping breath. This was just the desired reaction I was seeking. I am Jack's smirking delight.

"Wake up, Biff, we're ready for your closeup!" I spray him again, directly hitting his eyes this time, score another point for me!

"Stop, please, what the fuck are you spraying me with, you psycho bitch?"

"Piss, Biff, I figured it was fitting for a human toilet bowl like yourself."

Biff struggles momentarily before he fully realizes the serious predicament, he finds himself in.

"What is all of this?" is all he can manage to say before he trails off into silent bewilderment.

"What this is, Biff, is what we in the snuff business like to call a bind. And boy, howdy, are you ever in one now, bubba!"

"I don't understand why I am here."

"Oh, poor baby," I say in a mocking tone.

"You rapist fucks never know why, do you? If I had a dime for every predator that told me the exact same thing, I would have a shit load of dimes, let me tell you. Well, let's pretend that you are truly clueless then, shall we? You like to fuck girls in their ass, either by tricking them, drugging them, or outright raping them. That's an exit only, Biff, unless the girl is into it, of course. But guess what? All the girls' you sodomized weren't into it in the slightest. So, eventually the word got to me from my fanbase, and voilà, here you are in my web, little fly. As you can see, if you struggle too hard, you're going to take a nasty spill!"

Biff looks at my trap for him, finally understanding the gravity of the situation he finds himself in. He sits atop of a small, wooden platform that teeters precariously with every movement. Both of his arms and legs are being weighed down by two cinder blocks, tied to each of his appendages, for a total of eight blocks. At thirty-five pounds a pop, that's two-hundred and eighty pounds trying to pull his worthless ass towards his comeuppance. The ropes are heavily digging into his flesh, causing his skin to redden; it's even beginning to weep blood from the friction caused by the itchy, coarse material of the rope.

"Now, all I have to do is use this chain connected to your wooden platform, and pull it out from under you, sending you to your true fate. Would you like to know what's under the platform, asshole? That's a rhetorical question by the way, I don't care what you want! Have you ever seen the film Cannibal Holocaust, Biff? No? That doesn't surprise me, you seem like a total Chad, so I doubt you like anything cool. Anyways, Cannibal Holocaust is probably the very first found footage film that came out, years before The Blair Witch Project. In the film, a group of people go to the Amazon rainforest to do a documentary on cannibal tribes, only to never be heard from again. Their video equipment is eventually found though, and it turns out, they staged a lot of horrific scenes just so they could have provocative footage. Ultimately, the Amazonians rise to their American oppressors, and they are killed and eaten by the cannibal tribe. Well, arguably, one of the most iconic scenes is of a woman that is skewered from vagina to mouth on a big wooden spike. Want to take a wild guess on what is under that platform you are sitting on, Biff?"

Biff begins to shake in fear as the dire situation hits him like a ton of bricks.

"BINGO! That's right, anal rape boy, I think you're finally getting the er, point, get it!" He doesn't laugh at my awesome dad joke, but that's ok, I'll do the cackling for the both of us.

"Any parting words before I get this shit show on the road?"

"I don't deserve to die for what I did."

"Oh, really?"

"No this is crazy; I have parents and people who love me. So, I fucked some girls in their asses. Some liked it, some didn't. It shouldn't be an immediate death sentence."

I look at Biff like he is an exotic deep-sea creature that has just been discovered, I even give him a head tilt like I'm Michael Myers or Jason Voorhees.

"Well, this is where you are wrong, chump. Did you know just the other day the Taliban blew an Afghan woman's brains out just for not wearing a burqa? People get killed over frivolous shit every single fucking day. You are not exempt; you are not special. You said you're loved? Who gives a fuck? That's no reason to keep your toxic ass on this Earth to continue to do as you please to women. They might not be able to get vengeance on you, but I can. And guess what? Nothing makes me happier than to crush you all like the insignificant bugs you all are."

Biff says nothing back. All he does is lower his head in total defeat and cry very softly to himself. It feels better than sex when I break a man's spirit. It's akin to killing them twice in my eyes. It's the ultimate power, to take someone's life. In these all too brief, fleeting moments I truly feel God-like.

With an all too obvious and nefarious glee, I began to pull the chain in earnest. Biff continues to cry but does not try to make a plea for his miserable life again. I guess he has chosen to die a man instead of a mewling baby. I didn't see that coming from him, his ilk usually are nothing more than children disguising themselves as adults. Kudos to Biff, I guess. I am at the precipice of the chain, one more tug should do it, and seal this fucker's fate.

With a knowing wink, I mug for the camera, and announce, "IT'S SHOWTIME!"

I pull the chain once more, with all my might, sending the platform crashing somewhere far behind me. For a moment, Biff just hovers in the air, like Wile E. Coyote in those old Road Runner cartoons from my youth. Then, gravity takes ahold of Biff in its deadly embrace and brings him crashing down hard on the incredibly sharp point of the enormous stake. It easily excavates its way deeply inside of his overly stretched anal cavity. Biff's frenzied screams and bellows of pain creates a huge wall of sound. He is almost as loud as the brutal tearing sounds of his meat as it is violently ripped to shreds. Biff's rectum and colon are almost immediately skewered, and decimated, as is his small intestines. Shit, and an almost oil-black blood, jettison out of his ruined asshole like a geyser, covering everything below him with a blood and feces concoction.

The spike is easily laying waste to Biff innards and vital organs, crushing everything in its path like an iron fist pummeling through his insides, as it travels upwards towards its ultimate destination. In Biff's final moments, he looks skyward, as if half expecting to see God watching all of this transpire from his lofty spot up in the Heavens. Just as he does that, the spike violently erupts out of his throat, bursting capillaries, and causing his neck to swell to a ridiculous, painful level. It then discharges out of his mouth, spraying gallons of blood, organs, teeth, and even a dislodged section of his heart ventricle skyward like a mini explosion. Biff's death throes help the spike ascend further as his gore-soaked, ruined asshole slides further down its girth. Blood pumps out frenetically after the jugular is laid open from the spike's sharpened point.

As it finally exits from the human Biff-kabob, blood seeks evacuation from every conceivable unplugged orifice, flowing out in rivulets. It rains down on me like a lovely, warm spring shower. I slowly dance in it as I begin to lather my body with his plasma. I'm feeling a little turned on to be honest. I look up at Biff in all his newfound glory. He looks like a beautiful work of art now. Created not with paint and brushes, but with gore and blood. He continues to stare at the skies with sightless, dead eyes. In fact, the pressure was so great, that his eyes almost popped out of their sockets entirely, bulging out like a pug, only a million times more severe, and not nearly as cute.

I must admit I wasn't prepared when I looked down to Biff's groin to see a steady stream of plasma pouring out of his dick hole, like he was urinating blood from the most severe case of UTI that ever existed. Without thinking, I grabbed a shot glass, and held it underneath his spurting phallus until it filled it up with his dwindling life fluid. Then I threw it back, just like an actor in those old timey westerns used to do.

With a burp, and a backhanded wipe of my mouth, I exclaimed, "Now that really hit the spot!"

I felt like the video was good, but I wanted to give the fans a bit more carnage candy for their bucks; it's what my audience clamors for after all. Go big or go home, right??? So, with that, I reached up and grabbed Biff's legs, and proceeded to drag him the rest of the way down to the ground, just for sadistic shits and giggles. I quickly discover though, that the spike is now like a cork in a wine bottle, meaning he's firmly stuck in place by the immense pressure. I mean, Biff is stuck harder than my nipples get when I stuff my hairy muff with maggots! Geez, this rapist pig is really going to make me work my sexy ass off to get this scene perfect. Well, I do aim to please!

I go back over to my gore-streaked worktable and select a razor-sharp butcher's knife. It gleams in my firm grip from the harsh lights of my killing room floor. I begin to hack into Biff's chest with fervor, cutting in a downward motion, using an ample amount of elbow grease to ensure I get this job done. After I emit some grunts, like I'm a lunk-head deadlifting an impossibly heavy weight in the gym, my efforts finally begin to pay off. With the knife buried in deep to the hilt, I savagely saw the rest of the way down his pathetic, bulbous gut, down to his pubic region. That's where my bloodlust reaches a ghastly crescendo. With a groan of unholy desire, I fling the bloody knife to the floor, and begin to rip the remaining ligaments free with my bare hands. When that doesn't work, I use my incisors, and chew what little sinews are left holding his mangled, worthless frame together like a starving coyote.

With one final ferocious tear, Biff's body finally splits apart like a shattered China plate, spilling its gruesome contents upon me as well as the floor. Steaming ropes of his gooey intestines emerge from his newly created orifice, like angry serpents awakened from their long slumber, and plummet to the ground with a moist and juicy splat. I pilfer inside of his husk with zeal, extracting his lungs, kidneys, and even Biff's heart. My crimson-coated hands gently lob each newly excommunicated organ to the ground, joining his innards, forming a giant meat pile. I jump into them like a child jumping into a pile of raked leaves. I even manage to make a beautiful blood angel with his plentiful gruel that is coagulating on my floor.

Biff's brain is all that remains on the spike, deeply imbedded on the tip, like a grisly variation of corn on the cobb, just like my mom used to make. My Redroom has never been more aptly titled; it resembles a slaughterhouse at the end of a busy work shift. Viscera, blood, shit, and gastric juices cover the floor, like candy from a smashed pinata at a kid's birthday party.

Now, this is how you kill a worthless piece of shit. I look to the camera, wink, and in my best Porky the Pig impression I say, "Th-Th-That's All Folks!"

# Chapter Fifteen

# Kim's Plan Is A Go

I look at my phone and see that Seth is calling. I have been pacing around my hotel room in anticipation for his callback. My blood is still boiling knowing that Morticia killed my brother, and is out living her life, while only God knows where Tanner's dead body is rotting away at. I can't even give him a decent burial. I will get my answers though, she will tell me everything I want, as I'm slowly cutting pieces off her just for fun. Just the thought of carving Morticia up like a Thanksgiving turkey is the only thing keeping me going lately. Seething, I walk over to my phone and answer it.

"This better be good, Seth, I am in a vendetta kind of mood, and anyone can get my wrath right now."

"Trust me, Kim, this is the news that you have been waiting for. Your plan is a go. I will have my people "capture" you at the drop off point. You'll be blindfolded and taken to the Hurt 2 The Core compound. I also managed to get you selected for that giant, mutated freak, Lurch, count your blessings you didn't end up in Pat Bale's hands."

"I can manage myself, thank you very much, Seth."

"You misunderstand, Kim," exclaims Seth. "That retard will be easier to get the drop on, is all I meant. Bale is no simpleton, plus he likes to dissect women and is utterly insane."

"I don't give a fuck who I end up with, to be honest, Seth, either one is already a dead man walking. They just don't know it yet."

"I don't doubt that, Kim, I know you are quite capable of handling yourself. I was only trying to help make sure you can achieve your objective is all."

"Thanks, but I'm going to attain my goal no matter what they throw at me. I'll feed each one of those bastards their own genitals before they even know what the hell is happening to them."

"Of course, Kim, I have no..."

I hit end before Seth can kiss my ass some more. I don't need to hear his empty platitudes of what he thinks I want to hear. I'm not a child and I do not need my ego stroked, especially from a man. I have prepared for everything, except for one thing, and that is how I am going to sneak a weapon into this Lurch's Redroom. The intel from Seth clearly dictates that my anus or vagina will not be an option for concealment, since his modus operandi is turning female genitals into mincemeat. If the big freak of nature gets that far with me, then my mission will be a total failure, both in terms of revenge, and being among the living. So, what's the next option?

I wrack my brain for possibilities in terms of weaponry. I need something that is concealable but can still inflict damage that is difficult to repair. I walk into the kitchen to fix myself a scotch on ice. I get a glass, and I walk over to the drawer to retrieve my ice pick, and stare at it in my hands as an idea begins to form. An ice pick would be a fantastic choice to surprise this big bastard. I mean, if Sharon Stone can kill with it, then why not me, right? I could stab him half a dozen times before he even knows what is happening. I'll have him bleeding internally with no possible way for him to close the wounds. I'll just need to make sure that I continuously stab, and twist the tool as I attack him, and I will have this monstrosity begging me to stop; he will be malleable putty in my hands. All I need to do now is sheath it in a safe spot that is easily accessible for me but not in a spot where this creature can find it first.

And that's when I get an absurd, yet oddly ingenious, epiphany. I look at my right forearm since my left is my dominant, strong hand, and decide on an incision site to insert the ice pick. I look inside my drawer, and pilfer around the clutter, until I stumble upon my scalpel in its case. I also find a rubber protective tip from a pair of scissors so I can cover the sharp end of the ice pick, so I don't nick anything vital, while it hides beneath my epidermis. I take some alcohol, pour it on the scalpel blade, and proceed to cut into my flesh. Blood steadily ekes from the wound as I continue slicing, unfazed, another benefit of not being able to feel pain. I make sure to stay in the outermost layer of my epidermis, in my forearm, and avoid entering the dermis.

The illusion must only work for a little while, and from what intel I have gathered, the buffoon I am being delivered to, is apparently a few sandwiches short of a picnic, so I should be just fine. With a deep breath, I push the tool into my forearm with my right pointer finger, until the ice pick is fully hidden under my skin. It's not perfect but it isn't all that noticeable unless you are specifically looking for it. I grab a thread and needle from my miscellaneous drawer, and commence to giving it a few stitches, just to hold the illusion in place. With a curt nod to myself, I approve of the half-assed stitch job, take a drink of my scotch, and contemplate my game plan.

With any luck, by tomorrow night, I will be looking Morticia Maggot dead in her eyes, while I gut her like a fish. God help anyone who tries to get in my way, because I will leave a pile of corpses in my wake without any hesitation whatsoever. I might not make it out of this alive after all the smoke clears, but neither will she, and I'm okay with that. I take another drink from my glass, and prepare a hot bath, possibly for the very last time.

# Chapter Sixteen

# An Insidious Plan

I guess the age-old adage, wanting what you can't have, isn't a load of bullshit after all. I mean, I can have any woman I want, any night of the week, to do with as I please. That usually entails sticking needles into their breasts, and nipples, creating makeshift pin cushions. Or rubbing a cactus against their genitals, shredding it to a bloody pulp before I insert it deep inside of their ruined cunt holes, but I digress. You probably think that I am a pretty sick guy. But you? I can't even catch your eye. I only seem to obtain your complete and utter disdain.

All you seem to care about is hanging out with that over-sized doofus Lurch and reading your crummy Splatterpunk books. Maybe killing your male victims too, but that seems to be it in my eyes. I like to mentally undress you while I'm lurking around the compound, making sure I stay just out of your peripheral vision. I imagine seeing you nude in front of me, covered in raw meat, being feasted upon by a swarm of writhing maggots, and my cock turns to stone. I read your infamous blog and found it oddly sensual that you filled your pussy with maggot-littered rotten meat and fucked yourself to a full-blown orgasm with a severed, rotting deer hoof. You almost died from indulging in your fetish; that's admirable to me.

This level of sadism in a woman absolutely astounds me. It's what made me fall in love with you, I'm not too ashamed to admit it. I mostly fantasize about bisecting your body parts, slowly and painfully, or French-kissing a freshly created orifice I've cut into you before I fuck it, but I have on a few occasions, had a totally pedestrian sex fantasy about you. I know, crazy right? Here's something I bet you didn't know, Morticia. I have been tracking your schedule for weeks now, on the down low. All your daily rituals, I have mentally tucked away.

You are so predictable; did you know that? I've been doing this for one sole purpose. Tonight, Morticia my sweet, you are all mine, and I am going to do whatever I please to you. I think after I am finished fucking, and then butchering your carcass, maybe I'll partake in some cannibalism? I would delight in eating your breasts, and vagina, especially after being pan-seared and garnished with cilantro and lime.

I feel like it would be a thrill to be the one thing that finally ends your miserable existence. I know that at the end of the day, you truly want to die, and I am more than happy to oblige. I will do it much more efficiently than you can. I see your past brushes with death in your blog entries as a cry for help, nothing more than the equivalent of a palsied old man's clumsy attempt at grasping a tool he desperately needs but cannot grip. Let me be that tool now, Morticia.

I will accomplish what you have been desperately trying to do your whole life. The road you've chosen has led you directly to my outstretched arms. I will give you the death you truly deserve. A death that everyone will remember, once they've seen it. I will record it and upload for all to see. I plan on making it my best work to date. I'll be incorporating pain meds, adrenaline, and other narcotics to ensure I keep you alive for the longest time possible, so I can do your demise the justice it truly deserves.

I will make it a true work of art. Once, I kept a fifteen-year-old girl alive for an entire day, even though I slowly used a blowtorch on her more tender parts. Her body looked like a spent, blackened piece of bacon, long forgotten on a burning grill by an inebriated father on the Fourth of July. By the time her literal flame extinguished, it took two weeks to air out that burnt flesh, scorched hair smell. But the visuals of watching her clitoris first shrivel from the immense power of the flame, then blacken to a charcoal nub, before crumbling off her crotch into dust will stay with me forever. I want your demise to eclipse everything I have done in the past, Morticia, you deserve that much.

I anticipate Lux will be less than pleased. I'm sure I'll get chewed out, but I've been chewed out by the best of them. I'm not one to play by the rules or listen to authority figures. I'm sure there will be repercussions, but the risk is, oh, so worth the reward. The only thing I need to be careful about is Lurch. That retarded bastard is connected to you at the hip when you aren't working. I know tonight is my chance, since tomorrow is your usual movie night, and you are always up late. Tonight, is an early turn in night for you both. I'll have over eight hours of alone time with you, Morticia, before anyone even knows there is a problem.

Once Lurch finds out what I have done to his precious girl, I'm sure he will want to kill me, but Lux won't allow that. I am the star here; I make six figures on nearly every cheese pizza film I complete for this place. I'm a legend in the underground. So, maybe I will just strike him fast and hard with my trusty stiletto knife and leave him trying to stop his intestines from falling out of his gut before his stupid ass even knows what hit him. Lux will just have to find some new talent. It's his fault anyway for hiring you in the first place; I warned him right off the bat not to hire a woman, but did he listen? It's his fault, not mine. I can't be held accountable for being myself. I mean, do we blame the shark for attacking the surfer? I don't think so.

*\*\**

I sneak into the compound's main rec room, making sure to stay cloaked in the darkness, as I set my sights on Morticia and Lurch finishing their dinner. They should be at ease, since typically they would be the only people here on a Tuesday night. They certainly wouldn't expect me to be here! I watch as the giant retard gives her a hug as they head off to their respective bedrooms. I often wonder if Lurch loves her romantically, and the thought causes me to chuckle involuntarily to myself. For one, he is probably the most hideous creature that ever existed; he wasn't just hit by the ugly stick, he was beat with it until it broke into a million pieces. He looks like the stuff of nightmares. Nothing could possibly receive love looking like he does. The next deal breaker for him is the size of his cock. Obviously, his gigantism affected all of his body, I've seen his cock split a regular woman's vagina in two like it was made of wrapping paper. It's a stupendous sight to behold. No woman has ever survived being penetrated by Lurch.

One time, years ago, they had Lurch fuck a cow for a bestiality video for a client. I watched as his elephantine appendage had the animal screeching in pure agony as he fucked it to death. When he pulled out of her distended cunt, his dick was covered in gore. His copious sperm poured out of her destroyed orifice, along with what appeared to be dislodged portions of a baby calf, that was apparently aborted from the furious fucking the mother had just endured. It's kind of sad when I step back and think how lonely of an existence his life must truly be. And I'm preparing to kill his only friend? Yeah, I will have to assassinate him before he finds out what I am about to do.

I watch as they head off to their rooms, unaware of what is about to happen tonight. Nothing feels better than the sense of holding someone's life in your hands. When you're the physical embodiment of chaos, which I am, it makes you feel like Thanos wearing the Infinity Gauntlet, truly godlike in every conceivable way. The arousal I'm experiencing right now is almost too much to handle. Precum is already flowing from my unyielding cock in anticipation for tonight's festivities.

This will truly be a night to remember!

# Chapter Seventeen

# Dry-gulched

I give Lurch a big hug and tell him goodnight. I remind him that tomorrow is our movie night, and to be thinking of something for us to watch. He wants something scary, and I am so down for that. I watch him lumber off to his quarters, and I can't help but smile as I tear up a little for the big guy. I've never met someone with a heart as pure as his. I bet it is as big as the rest of him. That sentence seems silly in my head knowing what he does here, but Lurch never lets what he does at the compound affect any other aspect of his life.

The love I feel from him, and feel for him is gargantuan in size, much like the big guy himself. He needs me and the feeling is mutual. He turns before he enters his room and waves goodbye with a smile. I reciprocate the same and he heads off to bed. I turn toward my door, and fish my key out of my pocket to unlock my entry, but in doing so I drop them to the floor. Cursing under my breath, I kneel to pick them up off the ground. As I begin to stand up, my Spidey sense starts tingling like crazy, warning me that something is rotten in Denmark. Before I can turn around to survey my surroundings, I hear an all too familiar voice speak from behind me.

"Will you walk into my parlor, said the spider to the fly."

Before I can respond, I feel something very hard strike my head, and everything goes pitch-black.

# Chapter Eighteen

# In The Spider's Web

I awake to see Pat Bale's stupid face leering at me like a kid on Christmas morning, which must make me his present. I look down to see I am strapped in his gynecologist's chair, which I'm positive doesn't bode well for me. I tug at my restraints, but they hold me firmly in place. No half-assing it there, I see. I mean, I know he has been creeping on me every now and again, and he totally has been giving me some rapey eyes to boot, but I had no way of knowing this was in the cards. I am Jack's complete and utter surprise.

I must figure a way to bide some time on this asshole so I can figure out an escape plan. Knowing Pat, I'm sure he wants to torture me and do all kinds of sick shit to my lady parts, but hopefully he doesn't want to rape me though; that thought is more repellent to me than the idea of being viciously torn apart. I watch as he wordlessly walks over to where he keeps his vast array of weaponry, chooses a scalpel and brandishes it in front of me menacingly.

"Wondering what I am about to do to you, Morticia?"

"Nope."

"Cool as a cucumber until the end, huh?"

"I guess."

I watch his smile begin to spoil momentarily at the corners. It's a gamble but I'm hoping that playing the tough girl part will give me some time to think.

"One for you, Morticia! I've been curious what you look like in the nude, so I am going to cut off these pesky clothes you are wearing! Are you still going to try and play the 2 coolio 4 skoolio, girl?"

"If this is how desperate you are to see me nude, then go for it, Pat. I'm in no way able to stop you from being a wretched, lecherous fuck, as you can see."

I watch as he licks his lips like some cartoon wolf on TV from my childhood. He begins to slice my clothing off with obvious zeal and excitement. I didn't even know the psychotic bastard was into me like that. Talk about getting grossed out; gag me with a fork!

The sharp blade of the scalpel makes quick work of my clothes and before you can say "*sexual harassment*," I'm in my bra and panties. I stare at my captor as he ogles me up and down so many times, it would be almost comical if my situation wasn't so dire. I guess besides a gruesome death, I can look forward to some rape to boot! I am in some deep shit. With two more flicks of his trusty razor, he removes my bra and panties, leaving me as nude as the day I was born. The toxic cunt's lascivious grin widens to an almost impossible width, reminding me of an animated DC movie with the Joker I saw once.

Pat looks truly insane right now. It makes me ponder the numerous girls that have been snuffed out by his murderous hands. The thought of dying while those intense, soulless eyes bore holes through you would be truly a terrifying way to go. He continues to stare at my body like one would gawk at a mangled corpse after a horrific car wreck.

"Take a picture, it will last way longer, creepo."

"Does filming it count?"

I want to slap that smug grin off his face, but I am bound and helpless. I am not used to being powerless and it is infuriating to put it mildly. Pat traces his fingers almost lovingly on my thighs before he speaks again.

"I love how white your complexion is, almost translucent, actually."

"Thanks, you know how us Goth bitches are, the sun is a no-no, and I'm trying to be the physical embodiment of Lydia Deetz."

He smiles at my little Beetlejuice reference, which causes me to inwardly breathe a sigh of relief. Maybe I can bide some time before he goes all American psycho on my ass. He once again starts to traverse my body with his hands, and I can't keep from cringing due to his clammy, clumsy pawing. He unexpectedly parts my legs, spreading my labia apart with his fingers. For a moment, he dips a digit deep inside of me, removes it with an audible *pop*, and sticks his finger into his mouth, tasting me with a look of utter euphoria etched across his face.

"I had a feeling you'd be rocking the bush, and you taste as delectable as I imagined you would in all of my fantasies."

"I like having pubic hair, shaved pussies are for normie porno addicts, and filthy, degenerate child molesters, like yourself, Pat."

In hindsight, that was a stupid remark; baiting him when he has all the leverage was a bad move. His face darkens to the hue of bricks. He reaches out to my right nipple, yanking and twisting it with all his might, causing me to thrash about and yelp in pure agony.

"You might want to watch your mouth, cunt. I'm Willy Wonka and you are in my chocolate factory, remember that." Then he does the same to my other nipple, just for spite. That does it, this prick has me seeing red now. I am Jack's fury!

"What a tough guy," I mock. "Untie me and let's see what happens to your woman-hating ass. Don't take out your sick, incestuous mommy issues on me, little baby!"

"Sorry, Morticia, but I am not going to give you a chance, I know you're a dangerous woman. View this as a compliment to your savagery and take solace in the fact that you never had a chance against me."

I'm getting scared now, it is obvious I can't talk my way out of this situation. Still, I try and power my way through this *FUBAR* situation I am in.

"Lux is going to be furious, you know that, right? Not to mention that Lurch will tear your ass limb from bloody limb. You are still in a spot where we can just forget about this and pretend that nothing happened. You have my word."

*Wink-Wink,* I think to myself. Your ass is the grass, fuck-face, and I'm the motherfucking lawnmower, if I somehow survive the night!

"I can handle Lux, don't fret about it. I will get chewed out to be sure, but at the end of the day it won't matter. I'm the star here, I'm the untouchable one. And as for your retarded sidekick, I am going to have some fun with you, and then I am going to sneak into his room and snuff him out in his sleep. That giant freak could sleep through a fucking tornado and wouldn't even know it."

He is not wrong about Lurch; he has horrible sleep apnea and snores like a damn freight train. The thought of poor, sweet Lurch going out like that enrages me yet again, and I slam against my restraints in frustration.

"Don't touch a hair on his head, you worthless piece of puke," I spit vehemently.

"I think you should worry more about yourself right now, Morticia. Besides, you are both as good as dead by morning, regardless. Your spirits can be besties in Hell, if there is such a place, for all of eternity, for all I care."

I'm flabbergasted right now. I am up shit's creek, and I don't even have a fucking paddle. I'm so hyper focused on my quandary that I don't notice that Pat is talking to me. Only after he slaps the shit out of my face do I snap out of my mental conundrum.

"Pay attention to me when I talk to you and give me the damn respect I deserve! I was saying before you zoned out that I think I want to mark my territory. You are fine with me carving my name into your supple flesh, right? You are my property now, after all."

I stare at him dumfounded. The glee he takes in all of this is truly nauseating, but not surprising. In a world of politically correct humans, Pat Bale is a literal Tyrannosaurus Rex that somehow managed to elude walking into the nearest fucking tar pit, either from sheer luck or pure stupidity. A Neanderthal throwback to a time where full blown toxic masculinity was the norm. It's jarring to know that a man exists in this world that hates women on a level as severe as this.

I sometimes ponder why he has such disdain for vaginas. He takes such pride in coming up with new and inventive ways to dismantle our female anatomies. It's like he is almost afraid of ladies and the power that our bodies have over men. A psychiatrist would probably have a field day taking a deep dive into his twisted psyche, I'm sure of that.

"You're not really asking permission, Pat, so let's cut the shit, okay? You are going to do whatever that black thing in your chest you call a heart desires. So, get to carving me up or shut up about it already."

"As you wish, milady," he purrs with faux respect.

"Now, where would my John Hancock look best? Maybe on your perky ivory titties, or how about right above that sweaty, luscious bush of yours?"

"Gee, I don't know, both spots sound so enticing, if you ask me," I exclaim in mock excitement.

"Let's let a coin flip decide. Heads, it's your breasts, or tails, it's the pubic area."

I watch him fish a quarter from over on his workstation and fondle it with reverence before giving it a mighty flip into the air. We both watch in fascination as the coin soars into the air, flipping end over end, before gravity takes control and brings it back down to his outstretched palm. He takes it and slaps it onto the top of his other hand and gazes at the outcome. A creepy, wry smile etches across his face like it was drawn on. He looks me dead in my eyes, blade gleaming, grinning manically.

"Let's carve up those perky tits of yours, shall we?"

# Chapter Nineteen

# A Bad Dream

I wake up with a start somethin' fierce! I had a terrible nightmare where I was jus' a lil' fly stuck in a big spider's web. I was strugglin' with all my might to get loose, but I only got more stuck! Then, a big ole hairy spider crept down and started spinnin' its web around me as it prepared to eat me right up. Right before it sunk its fangs into me, I look around and see Miss Morticia all spun up in the same web and hollowed out from the spiders feedin'. She was a goner, pale and unmoving. I looked at that dad-gummed bug with so much anger and it smiled at me and spoke in Mr. Bale's voice!

"I got your girl, dummy; you couldn't protect her. She is dead and so are you!"

Now, I never had a dream this terrifyin' before! I try to shake it off and get some more shuteye, but the dream left its hooks in me like I was a big mouth bass that me and my grandpappy used to catch on our property. I get up and stretch, my back pops till it's soundin' like I wuz makin' popcorn in the dadgum microwave! I yawn, scratch my gonads, and rise from my rat's nest of a bed. I was initially gonna drain my lizard and then try to get some more shut eye, but I decide to go to the kitchen area to get a drink. That way I could also check on Miss Morticia.

The nightmare is still bothering me. I wonder what it all meant! Why did the spider sound like Mr. Bale? Was the dream a *premernition*? I head to the toilet and kind of lean against the wall since my pecker is harder than a damned piece of rebar! After I gets myself situated, I let out a shower of urine from my aching' piss pump. I stand there drainin' the main vein for what seems like a zillion years, till the stream finally recedes into a trickle and then a drip. I shake it a couple of times, put it back into my pants, and head yonder into my room so I can put my slippers on and gets myself a sip of cold water, and check on Miss Morticia.

It's silly of me to be so spooked from a ridicerlous dream, but I love her and want to make sure she is ok. As I get outta my room, it's as quiet as a cemetery and just as dark to boot. The lights in the facility mostly go out at bedtime cuz of a timer, and only a few areas stay on 24/7. To conserve energy, I suppose. Its funny cuz this place makes a lot of dough, but they are some real tightwads, you know? I head out into the hallway towards the cafeteria area and pick my seat cuz my tighty whities are jammed all up in my ass pipe. Gosh, ain't that a sketch? I'm glad I'm alone cuz that is embarrassin' as all get out.

I finally make it to the kitchen area and grab myself a cup from the cabinet. I go to the sink and let the cold water run for a spell, then fill up my cup. Cold water sure is damned refreshin'! Well, since I had a might powerful thirst, I fill my cup up again and down it all in one big swallow. I belch and place the cup into the dish drainer since it ain't dirty cuz I only put water in it. I am fittin' to head back to bed but then the dream springs back into my mind again. Shoot! I almost forgot to check on my girl, my brain is so dumb! I begin to worry somethin' awful all over again! I decide to go and check on Miss Morticia just to be safe and to put my fretting noggin at ease. I head in the direction of her room as quickly as I can, but quietly too, so's I don't disturb her slumber. Miss Morticia can be quite the grouch if she doesn't get enough shuteye, lemme tell ya!

As I arrive at her door, I grasp the handle quietly and give it a turn and nuthin'! It's locked! She never locks the door at night. Now, I'm gettin' worried! What if she fell or somethin' and cracked her skull? I'm picturin' all types of horrible ideas and I begin rilin' myself up into a frenzy, so I decides to just break down the door even though I'll probably get in trouble tomorrow bout bustin' it to smithereens! I raise up my foot to the door handle and I put all my force into the kick. The door flies inwards like a stick of dynamite went off! I walks in and I'm stunned at what I am seein'. Mr. Bale has Miss Morticia all strapped up where she can't hardly move an inch. It was just like in the dream, it was a dad-gummed *premernition*! He has taken a sharp blade to her boobies and wrote *"PAT'S CUM RAG."* That's just damned disrespectful as all get out! Gross too!

The blood is still cascading down her round, perky breasts, but the worst part is that this sick son-of-a-bitch is lappin' at that blood like some kind of mangy mongrel, or a dad-gummed vampire! That's when both look directly at me. Miss Morticia looks happier than ever to see me, but Mr. Bale looks a might bit upset and scared to boot. I promised myself I would never let anything bad happen to my best friend. But I failed her! I have always been afraid of Mr. Bale but no more, I'm standin' up to him today and I am goin' to kill him for what he did!

I rush to him before he can make a move, and grip him in my arms, and lift him up to my face like he weighs nothin' more than a lil baby does. I roar into his face, causing his perfectly gelled hair to get all mussed up, and he cringes like a lil' scaredy cat. I now wonder whys I was afraid of this bully for so long? I guess it took him tryin' to hurt someone I really love to make me snap outta it. With him still in my arms, I slam him down to the ground with such force that I hear both of his femur's breakin' in half, when his feet hit the ground with a pleasant cracking sound, like kindling snapping and popping in a fire pit. Mr. Bale screams like he is getting the tar whooped outta him, which causes me to smile in satisfaction! Miss Morticia looks at me with a smirk that kind of scares me.

"Just in the nick of time, my knight in shining armor rescues his fair maiden!" She says to me.

"Aww shucks, tw'erent nothing."

"Bullshit, my friend. You just saved my life from this lewd fuck! But it's payback time now, so how about untying me so we can teach this creepy fuck a lesson he will never forget?"

"I likes the sound of that, Miss Morticia!"

# Chapter Twenty

---

# The Pain Game

After Lurch gets me loose from my restraints, I give him a big ole hug and a massive, sloppy kiss, embarrassing him in the process. Sometimes the world works in mysterious fucking ways, you know? If you would have told me that befriending a giant, redneck mutant would someday save my life, I would have laughed my ass off from the prospect of it. Probably would have slit your throat too! But here I am, saved from the claws of this hideous fiend, thanks to my hulkish guardian angel.

I look down at the perverted shit that this assclown carved into my previously perfect breasts, and I am fuming mad. As he was lapping up my blood like a bootleg vampire Lestat, he kept trying to fingerbang me, but his dirty, prying dick beaters dried up my cooch worse than the Sahara Desert! As if he could ever have a shot with me. For one, I'm way too hot for his ass. And for another, he is nothing but a dirty child fucker to boot! Kick rocks, motherfucker. We both look down at the ruined, splintered appendages that used to be Pat's legs, and giggle maniacally together like a couple of bratty, little kids. We also taunt his cries, mocking his ugly, crybaby face, just for spite.

Ample amounts of blood pour out of the holes that have torn open from his shattered femur bones, ripping new and exciting exit wounds from his demolished flesh. His shriek of palpable agony is the most beautiful music to my ears though; if I could play it on repeat, I would! I smile wickedly, watching as he writhes on the floor, like a criminal being tasered repeatedly by a corrupt centurion.

"What do you say we get this lump of human excrement onto the table, Lurch baby?"

"Whatever you want, Miss Morticia! You gonna hurt 'em good, I betcha!"

"That's the only way I do it, baby, I do it hard!"

The sexual innuendo goes over the big man's head, which is fine by me. I love that, my boy, though brutal in his films, is rather oblivious to things like that. He is truly a pure soul in essence. After all, he never asked for this life like the rest of us did. He was thrust into it out of survival, literally kill or be killed. After Lurch effortlessly throws Pat onto the table like the trash he is, he binds him to the gynecological chair with razor wire. I watch with pure malice on my grinning mug, while the blades hungrily dig their teeth into his skin and hold him rigidly in place.

"You gonna want me to help ya kill his devilish ass, Miss Morticia?"

"Aww, aren't you just the sweetest! Thanks, but no thanks, my boy, I think I got him right where I want him. You can run along back to bed. I think I'm going to have some fun with him before I put this cockroach out of its misery."

Lurch looks at me uncertainly and then at Pat.

"Is you sure?"

I cup his cheek lovingly in my right hand, look him right in his teary eyes, and say,

"Honey, he isn't going to be any more trouble for either of us ever again, I pinky promise!"

I put out my dainty pinkie to his monstrous one, and we literally do just that. I get on my tippy toes, kiss his bulbous forehead and tell him to go on, which he reluctantly does.

He gives me one last look before walking out of the room. I give him a smile, nod, and blow him a kiss, which he catches. He gives me a wan smile and leaves from my line of vision. Once I am sure Lurch has gone, I turn towards dickhead, and ominously glare at him. Pat opens his mouth to, no doubt, spew some bullshit lies to try and save his miserable ass, but before he can utter much more than a squeak, the hammer is already in my hands and I am pounding on his right kneecap with everything I can muster, which is a lot.

Pat's eyes bulge to cartoonish levels as he once again begins to wail in pure agony. I take my trusty hammer and beat the shit out of his left kneecap. I am Jack's raging vengeance. I raise the hammer yet again and bring it down full force onto his left elbow, then do the same thing to his right.

The bones eventually sound like smashed glass being shaken violently in a baggie. Once I have finished wailing on his punk-ass, I toss the bloody hammer into the corner of the room, and stare at this waste of life, shaking from pain, curled into a ball right before me. Incredibly, his cock is still as inflexible as ever, which can only mean one thing in my mind, so I ask.

"Did you take a bunch of boner pills or something, Pat?" He looks at me, and momentarily, the old Pat Bale comes back with full force. His eyes flash a sardonic gleam of pure hatred for me, causing me to fleetingly take a step back from him.

"Yeah, I took three tablets. I wanted to rape your cunt till it bled, you worthless, walking, cum dump."

And just like that, his momentary hold on me vanishes. His words are all he has left now, and we all know the song about sticks and stones breaking bones, but words can never hurt us. I see him for the pathetic weasel he is.

I smirk at this last-ditch effort of false bravado and say, "A tough guy till the end, I see. One for you, Pat!"

He doesn't say anything for a full minute, I guess he is pondering the fifth, but then he speaks again.

"You know if I get out of this, I'm going to make you suffer for the rest of your miserable existence, you Hot Topic, white trash cunt!"

"Oh, don't worry about getting out of this, you are as dead as Dillinger. But first, I want to play with that big, fat, juicy cock of yours!"

His terror is palpable now. He knows all about my dick mutilating reputation from my films. Not to toot my own horn but it's fucking legendary, toot-toot! I scan around his worktable and pilfer through his implements of hell, as he likes to lovingly call the tools of his murderous trade. But all the items I see would only expedite his demise. My appetite for destruction needs to be prolonged.

I am Jack's methodical and prolonged revenge!

I'm looking for something that can hurt him plenty, but also to lengthen his suffering for as long as possible. Then, I spy something with my little eye that will make things mighty spicy for this murdering, raping wretch. Pat watches in panic as I brandish my newfound weapon of choice. I can almost see the mechanics of his brain synapses firing, almost immediately guessing what I am about to do. Judging from his comical facial expressions, he is a million miles away from happy!

He is sweating profusely, and licking his lips uncontrollably, in total panic mode.

"Morticia, put that down please, I know I'm as good as dead, but please God, not that!" He begs.

I smile with false pity before I retort.

"Sorry, Pat, but hell hath no fury like a woman scorned, and you scorned the shit out of me! I guess you should have just left me alone. But guess what? I'm going to teach you a lesson you aren't ever going to forget!"

I take the length of sandpaper and wrap it around his blood engorged dick.

He bucks furiously against his restraints but to no avail. I shush him and begin to stroke him gently at first, like a lover might. I let him feel the friction at this slow and deliberate pace. It reddens and irritates his inflated genitals the second I begin stroking him off.

"Let's pick up the pace, what do you say, babyfucker?"

"No...Please...Stop!"

But I have no intention of stopping. This human shit stain has not only made my life troublesome here, but he has been nothing but a bully to Lurch for even longer. It is payback time! I jack him off with the sandpaper at a much quicker pace and the results on his cock are almost immediate.

His skin is already blistering from the paper's unforgiving texture. His screams and cries egg me on, causing me to pump his inflamed cock even faster. My hand kicks it up to a blistering speed, little fissures begin to erupt along the length of his tool, and start bleeding profusely, giving my tiring hand some much needed lube for assistance. The blistered parts of his shaft begin to tear open, leaving in its place the angry, red, unformed skin beneath.

Undeterred, I pump him with a renewed vigor. I watch in amazement as strips of his dick meat begin to come off from the unforgiving friction of the sandpaper. It reminds me of peeling the apple's skin off into strips as a child. The urinary meatus is streaming bountiful amounts of blood from its opening, as I continue to jackhammer his sandblasted sexual organ into oblivion. Without warning, the head of his cock explodes like an overcooked hotdog in the microwave. The head opens in four parts like a Morning glory flower at sunrise. It is so beautiful to behold!

Pat's dick looks totally alien now, like something out of an underground gore flick. The amount of blood still pouring out of its ruined head is staggering. Pat is shivering from the pain and looking extremely pale. I am on borrowed time now as he will not be in the land of the living much longer. I take a deep breath and look at his crotch region. It looks like a stick of dynamite was jammed deep into his dickhole, and I am gazing at the aftermath. I must admit this is hot as fuck. I begin to pinch my fully erect nipples, kneading my breasts with one hand, while I use my other hand to delve my finger into the ruined cavern of Pat's mutilated cock.

I am drenched to the core, so I begin viciously pawing at my lust filled, soaking cunt in a kind of sexual frenzy. My excessive vaginal fluids cascade down my thighs like water from a broken fire hydrant in the streets of the ghetto. I look at Pat as one might look at a dying possum in the road after striking it, a mix of indifference interlaced with curiosity. It is at that moment when I get an epiphany on the final coup de gras for his dying ass. A fitting end, no pun intended, to pure evil, trapped inside the form of a man. I use the ample amount of blood, and my abundant pussy juice, to lather up my hand and arm, then violently begin driving my forearm deep into Bale's virgin tight asshole.

His agonizing screams are as loud and as raucous as the fans at a Kansas City Chiefs game. The decibel level of his pained, vocal torment is astonishing to me. After I've forcefully stuffed all my fingers, then my whole hand inside of him; it feels extremely warm and comforting inside his orifice. This must be what it feels like to babies inside of their mothers' womb, I bet. Pat bucks and strains, after every inch that I push further inside of him, violating him just as he has done with every female he has ever met. Only now, I am the rapist. I push further than I thought possible, forearm deep inside of his anal cavity, and yet, I go further.

I am elbow deep inside of him as shit, and blood, begins to funnel out of his gape and tumbles down my arm as I fuck him with my appendage. It is when my shoulder prevents me from going any deeper inside of his impossibly gaping asshole, that my fingers wrap around his throbbing heart. I feel it beating frantically as he moans and gobbles incoherently. I grip it as tightly as I can and begin to reverse my hand out of Pat, as if I'm rewinding the scene on my DVR so I can enjoy it again and again.

As my hand continues down his body, heart in tow, I come to an abrupt stop. I must have gotten tangled up somewhere inside of him. With all my might, I yank ferociously until I feel his heart wrench free from its obstruction. I pull in earnest again, traversing through his innards with his heart tightly gripped in my hand, like a grisly trophy. Pat looks at me in what seems like total awe as his anus swells open to birth, and belch out my hand, and his still beating heart. An avalanche of shit and blood follow after.

I bring his organ up to my breasts and rub the gore-caked heart against my aching nipples as my other hand creeps to my sopping vagina, where I fingerbang myself, building towards a monstrous orgasm. Pat watches this all with a rapt fascination of lust-filled envy, even as his life essence disperses almost as quickly as his blood loss. He gazes deeply into my eyes and beckons me closer to him. He is saying something to me, but it is almost totally incoherent. His once boisterous voice is now just a shadow of its former self. For a fleeting second, I think this might be a ruse to get me closer so he can try some last-ditch effort at injuring me somehow, but then I laugh the thought away. I mean, I just pulled this loser's heart out of his fucking asshole, for Pete's sake! I mean, like c'mon, I won! So, I go to him, and let him whisper what he is trying to say into my ear. It's almost impossible to ascertain his words at first, but eventually it hits me.

"You are an amazing woman; I always knew you would be the death of me." He croaks out.

I give him my sexiest look and tell him, "Eat your heart out, loser." And as the light extinguishes from his devil eyes, I do just that, and take a great big bite.

# Chapter Twenty-one

# Up Shit Creek

I walk down the corridor to Lurch's room, knocking before I enter. He rises immediately from his bed. He looks as if he was having a conniption fit while waiting to see if I would live or die. I am still nude, and covered in Pat's blood, like it was some insane form of sheer negligée. Embarrassed, Lurch grabs his bedsheet and wraps it tightly against me as he hugs me for dear life. He looks down at my upturned face, his tears plopping onto my bloody visage.

"I was frettin' something fierce, Miss Morticia. I wanted to come help ya, but I did what you told me!"

"I told you I was a big girl and could handle myself, didn't I?"

"Yessum, you did indeed, I guess I don't ever need to doubt you, no more."

"I'm a woman of my word, Lurch my boy, I could whoop your butt if you make me mad enough!" I teasingly act like I'm going to hit him, and he cowers in mock fright, smiles back happily, and lets out a joyful "yee-haw," and says, "I don't doubt that!"

A serious look etches across his face a moment later.

"Is the dirty dog dead?" He asks.

"Oh yeah, Bale's dead, baby. Bale's dead. Want to go look at my light work?"

"Yessum, Miss Morticia, did ya' make a mess?"

"Lurch, who do you think you're talking to?" I tease with mock hurt, "I didn't just leave a mess; I left a fucking holocaust!"

"Woo doggy! Well let's go see this, Miss Morticia. You got me a might bit interested now, yes siree, Bob!"

And with that, we head off to look at the decimated corpse of Pat Bale, hand in hand. I let Lurch look at the aftermath by himself, staying in the doorway, and watching his expressions change like the colors on a chameleon. One minute he's smiling, and the next, he's grimacing. It is interesting watching the big man check out my work. When he has his fill of the depravity, he makes his way back to me.

"Gosh, Miss Morticia, you sure fucked him up!"

"Did I do a good enough job?" Smiling demurely as I ask.

"I's thinks too good almost! Sheeeeeit, that was gross, Miss Morticia! You opened a forty-gallon drum of whoop ass on that shitter, no doubt!"

In response, I dramatically bob a curtsy to him.

"Where's the rest of his heart?" Lurch asks.

In my best impression of Fat Bastard, I grab my stomach and say, "In my belly!"

Lurch's face is priceless at that moment, I think some of the color drained from it. All he can mutter is, "Goddamn," slowly shaking his head in total disbelief. We stand there in the silence for what seems like eons before Lurch speaks again.

"What are we gonna tell Lux, Miss Morticia? He's gonna know somethin's wrong tomorrow since it's Mr. Bale's day to film his nasty flicks!"

"We could always tell Lux that we took out the trash?"

"Not funny, Miss Morticia, we're in a heap of trouble!"

I shrug and head into the kitchen to grab myself a Coke Zero. Lurch lags somewhat behind at first, but easily ambles up to me in a flash. I open the fridge and fish out a can, draining it in one big, audible swig, and let loose of a belch that would make Booger from Revenge of The Nerds quake in his boots! Still feeling the euphoric effects of my epic murder of Pat, I jokingly quip, "Killing is awfully thirsty work, it would seem!"

I can see Lurch anxiously waiting for me to tell him that everything is going to be okay, but I know in my heart it won't be, and I'm not going to lie to my friend about it.

"I'm afraid we are probably in big trouble, buddy. Pat was worth a lot of money to this company; they are going to take it out of our asses." Lurch comically gulps in fright. It would be laughable if the big guy wasn't shitting his pants about our situation right now.

I put my hands on his shoulders lovingly and begin the arduous task of moving his enormous bulk to face me.

"I'm going to handle everything with Lux in the morning. I want you to stay in your room until I come and get you. Out of sight, out of mind, okay, pal?"

"Will they hurt us, yuh think?"

"To be honest, I am not sure what they are going to do to us. But if we have each other's backs, we should be alright. After all, we are a two-team wrecking crew and if we must fuck shit up, then so be it."

He nods, and I give him a big hug and shoo him off to bed. Once Lurch is gone, the realness of the situation finally sets in on me. The pep talk worked for the big guy but has left me an utter mess of jangled nerves and perspiring pits. I walk slowly to my bedroom, on legs that feel like they are made entirely of jelly. My brain begins to work in overdrive as I start to mentally try and figure out a way to get us out of this totally fucked scenario. Nearly the entire walk back to my quarters, I keep repeating this mantra silently to myself.

*Holy shit, we are so fucking fucked! I am Jack's crippling fear of what tomorrow brings for us...*

# Chapter Twenty-two

# Epilogue

The car that Seth arranged to bring me to the Hurt 2 The Core compound has just arrived in front of the motel that I'm staying at. Just like Seth told me, it was there promptly at eight o'clock that morning. The driver gives me a slight, courtesy honk, just to ensure that I realize he is outside. I take one last look around the sparse room, verifying that I gathered up the few belongings I have. As I grab my bag, my phone begins to vibrate. Irritatingly, I grab my phone and say, "I see you out there, give me a minute, okay?"

"Is that any way to speak to the person who is going to grant you the justice you seek for your brother, Kim White?"

I'm momentarily at a loss for words. I have absolutely no idea who I'm speaking with, but they already know way more about me, leaving me at a severe disadvantage.

"Who are you," I ask the mysterious caller.

"The name is Lux, my dear. Seth gave you up the minute you tried to choke him out and came up with that ridiculous plan of yours."

"Seth is a dead man," I fume.

"Already handled, my dear."

Befuddled by this whole conversation in general, and the genial tone of this murderous kingpin, I ask, "So why have a car come here if you know all about my ruse? Are you going to *whack* me or whatever you gangster types call it?"

"Don't be ridiculous, if I wanted you dead, you would have never awakened this morning. Now listen up...do I have your attention?"

"Yes, you have my total attention."

"Good. We had a bit of a falling out last night with my performers. Now, I must initiate a major cleanup. How big of a cleanup depends on what intel I get back from my two remaining entertainers. If I get the answer I'm hoping for, then it will be one great, big mess I'll need you to clean up for me."

I try and read between his cryptic lines, but he isn't giving me much. From what I can gather though, shit must have hit the fan there last night.

"What if it's an answer that you don't want to hear," I ask.

"Well, if that's the case, Kim, then not only will you be killing Lurch for his transgressions last night, but I will also give you the one thing that you so desire. Vengeance for your slain brother."

"Does that mean what I think it does," I ask, barely concealing my glee.

"It means that if she answers wrong, I will give you Morticia Maggot as well!"

TO BE CONTINUED...

# About The Author

Otis Bateman lives in Missouri where he writes his sick and depraved stories in his dilapidated trailer home.

He is creepy and disturbing. When he is not writing, he enjoys slasher, gore, and snuff films, especially snuff films.

He also enjoys watching random people sleep through their bedroom windows, late at night while tapping on the glass softly.

Printed in Great Britain
by Amazon